Otherland

Dide

AuthorHouse™
1663 Liberty Drive
Bloomington, IN 47403
www.authorhouse.com
Phone: 1-800-839-8640

© 2012 by Dide. All rights reserved.

No part of this book may be reproduced, stored in a retrieval system, or transmitted by any means without the written permission of the author.

Published by AuthorHouse   04/13/2012

ISBN: 978-1-4678-9024-3 (sc)
ISBN: 978-1-4678-9026-7 (hc)
ISBN: 978-1-4678-9025-0 (e)

Any people depicted in stock imagery provided by Thinkstock are models, and such images are being used for illustrative purposes only.
Certain stock imagery © Thinkstock.

This book is printed on acid-free paper.

Because of the dynamic nature of the Internet, any web addresses or links contained in this book may have changed since publication and may no longer be valid. The views expressed in this work are solely those of the author and do not necessarily reflect the views of the publisher, and the publisher hereby disclaims any responsibility for them.

Contents

Chapter 1	Strange Meeting	1
Chapter 2	Foreign Land	5
Chapter 3	Dreamed Trip	7
Chapter 4	On a Visit	11
Chapter 5	Unwound Yarn	15
Chapter 6	Those Fingers	19
Chapter 7	Pleasant Walking	23
Chapter 8	Awake while in Love	27
Chapter 9	Flying Device	31
Chapter 10	Fluctuating Clouds	35
Chapter 11	Wonderful Child	39
Chapter 12	Celebration	43
Chapter 13	Storm	47
Chapter 14	Flames of Joy	51
Chapter 15	Recognition	55
Chapter 16	Memories and Future	59
Chapter 17	The Sun's shadow	63
Chapter 18	Waking Up	67
Chapter 19	Smart Folly	71
Chapter 20	Easily Done	75
Chapter 21	Without Words	79
Chapter 22	The Narrator	83
Chapter 23	Something Unknown	87
Chapter 24	Refreshing Memory	91
Chapter 25	Ready to Sail	95
Chapter 26	Old Dreams	99
Chapter 27	The Time Lost	105
Chapter 28	A Journey Together	109

Epilogue 112

Dedicated to my mum, who filled my childhood with endless tenderness!

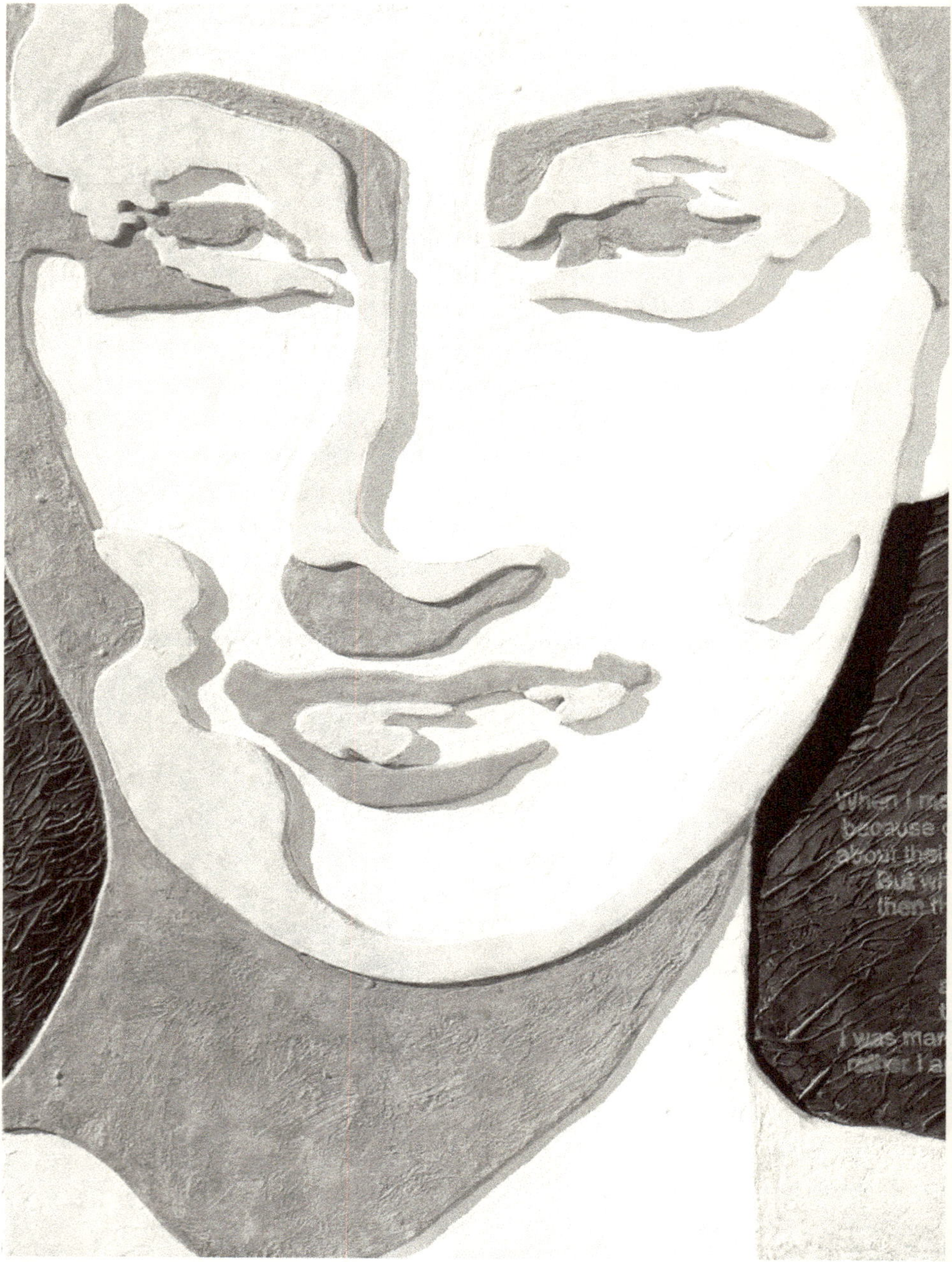

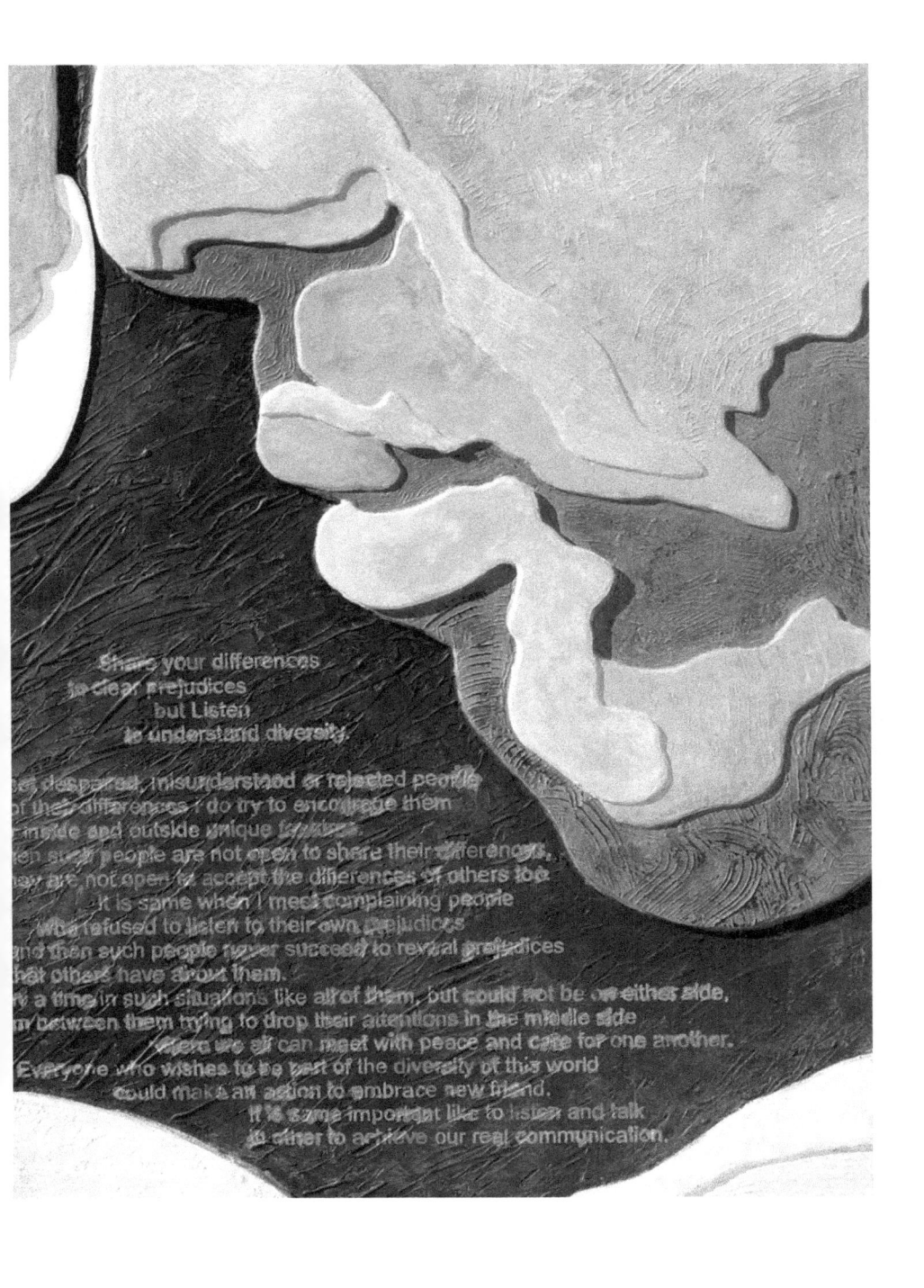

Share your differences
to clear prejudices
but Listen
to understand diversity.

When I have despaired, misunderstood or rejected people
because of their differences I do try to encourage them
of their inside and outside unique features.
When such people are not open to share their differences,
they are not open to accept the differences of others too.
It is same when I meet complaining people
who refused to listen to their own prejudices
and then such people never succeed to reveal prejudices
that others have about them.
I have a time in such situations like all of them, but could not be on either side,
I'm between them trying to drop their attentions in the middle side
where we all can meet with peace and care for one another.
Everyone who wishes to the best of the diversity of this world
could make an action to embrace new friend.
It is same important like to listen and talk
to other to achieve our real communication.

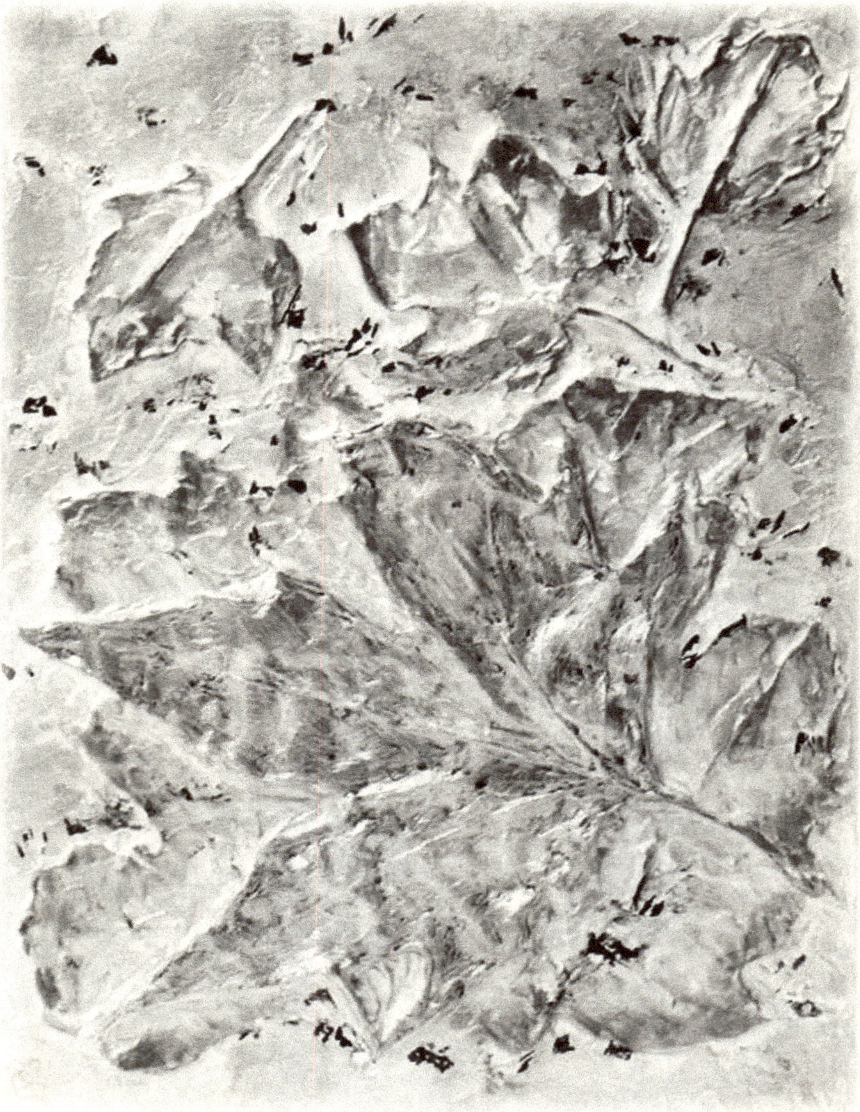

Aims are there for you to stand up for them, to pursue them, to fight for them or to kneel humbly for them; to shout out loud or to keep quiet, to let tears stream down your face, tears of joy or sorrow! When one has an aim, you negotiate with life, because you are not satisfied with what life throws at you; aims want to give birth to their own dreams and let them roam this world. They have already started passionately caring deep down for those dreams.

Then again, not all dreams make us equally happy. Only those that we conquer with love and they answer with love twice as strong which makes us truly happy.

It's a good idea to understand ourselves, to stop being bothered by what is small or big in other people's eyes and to care more about what fills our souls and makes us truly alive.

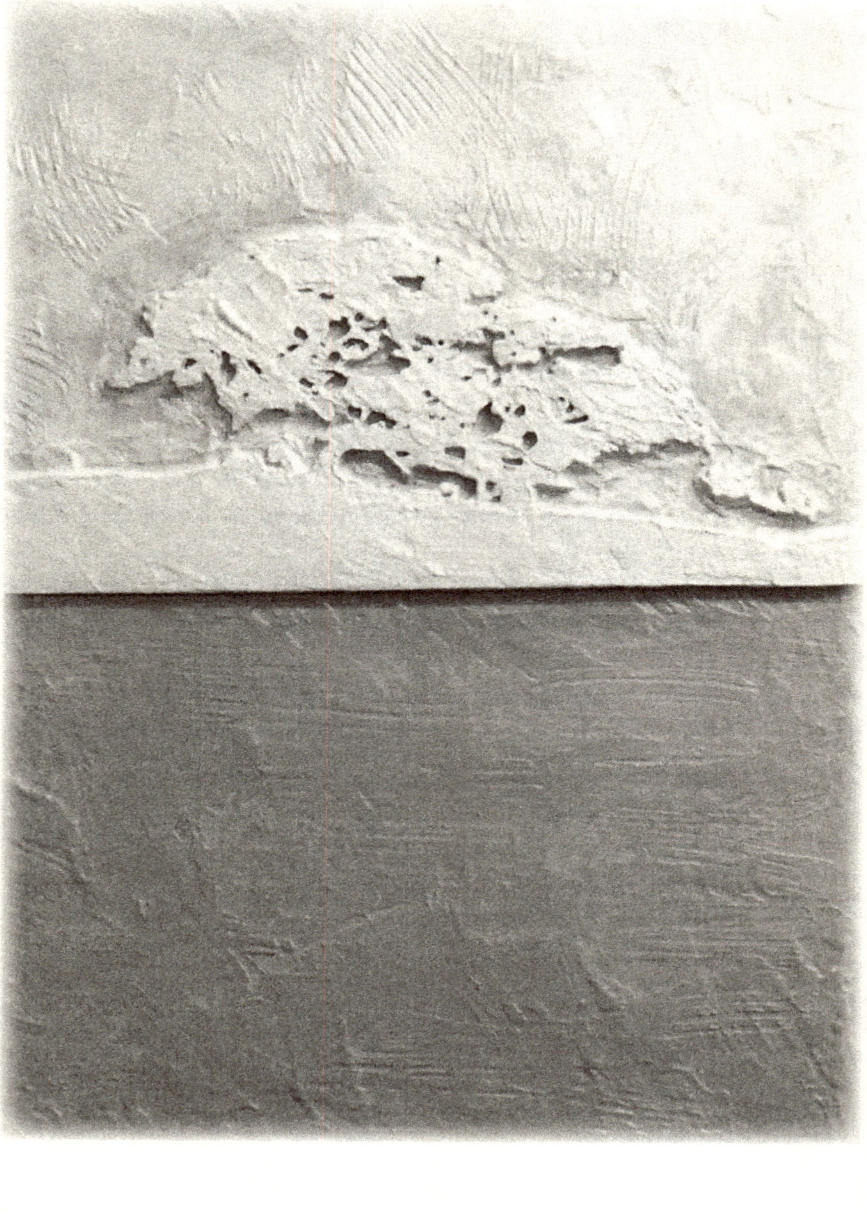

Chapter 1

Strange Meeting

Deep down in the depths of forgotten dreams, so far away and long ago, it seemed the memory came up again and began to shatter the illusion of her world. In her eyes there was a determination, perhaps mixed with some anger and bitterness. However, she believed that she would find a way to achieve these dreams. She decided to put them before her to see if they were possible, until they became her identity. This had to happen sooner or later, and running seemed to outrun the time to go after these dreams. So they became enemies, and this tortured her. She sought peace without resigning to fate, content with what she had.

She was not able to see any of those things, but was only running in the alley.

Meanwhile the sun thrust through the woods and toyed with the branches and leaves, so this captured her attention. And down in her mind appeared nothing, a reflected light from a simple game of sun and sky in the trees. Sometimes while embracing a goal, we meet someone who manages to leave something in us. We smile and then allow that it hardly fits into our plans. Instead we are left with something deep inside us. That was what happened to her that day.

While running, she lost her direction in her awakened thoughts, turned into a distracted girl, and wasted her thoughts rather than going on her way. Just then a voice stopped her. A boy noticed that one of her shoes was untied, so he called out to her casually to be careful not to stumble. When she turned, she saw a boy who walking carelessly, looking peaceful and absentminded. This made him more attractive against the backdrop of the sun. She smiled while bending down to tie her shoelaces. Her smile was like a magnet to him, making him stop for a moment on his walk.

Better collision than wandering! This he thought while his eyes were still focused on her smile that attracted all his attention. He felt happy in this moment watching this smiling girl busy with this little thing, just tying her shoelaces. He wanted to ask her something, but she forestalled him.

Was it a determination in her eyes to start a conversation or was it just her impulsive courtesy that prompted her to ask him where he came from? It appeared very strange to her for a native to be wasting his time in a place more commonly used by people on sightseeing tours or other purposes.

Her question did not surprise him. Rather he was glad, and said with relish that he wished first to kiss her and then he would answer her question. This was a raw joke for both, but they didn't seem to have understood, instead they decided to laugh in their audacity without exactly knowing why they did so.

She allowed herself to be kissed. And it wasn't just a mere kiss, but the beginning of a journey to a new world which she'd dreamt about a long time ago, a lost world that was a part of her. It was a world which always belonged to him, but at the same time was hidden deeply in her. Thus began the journey which neither expected. It was travelling that centred on asking questions. It was difficult for her to understand immediately what was really happening to her or to where this meeting would take her. For him it was a known way he had always passed, arriving finally in the place where they met.

At the time when she closed her eyes to be kissed, she saw herself on another planet. She couldn't quite understand how she found herself in this new world.

Dide

Otherland

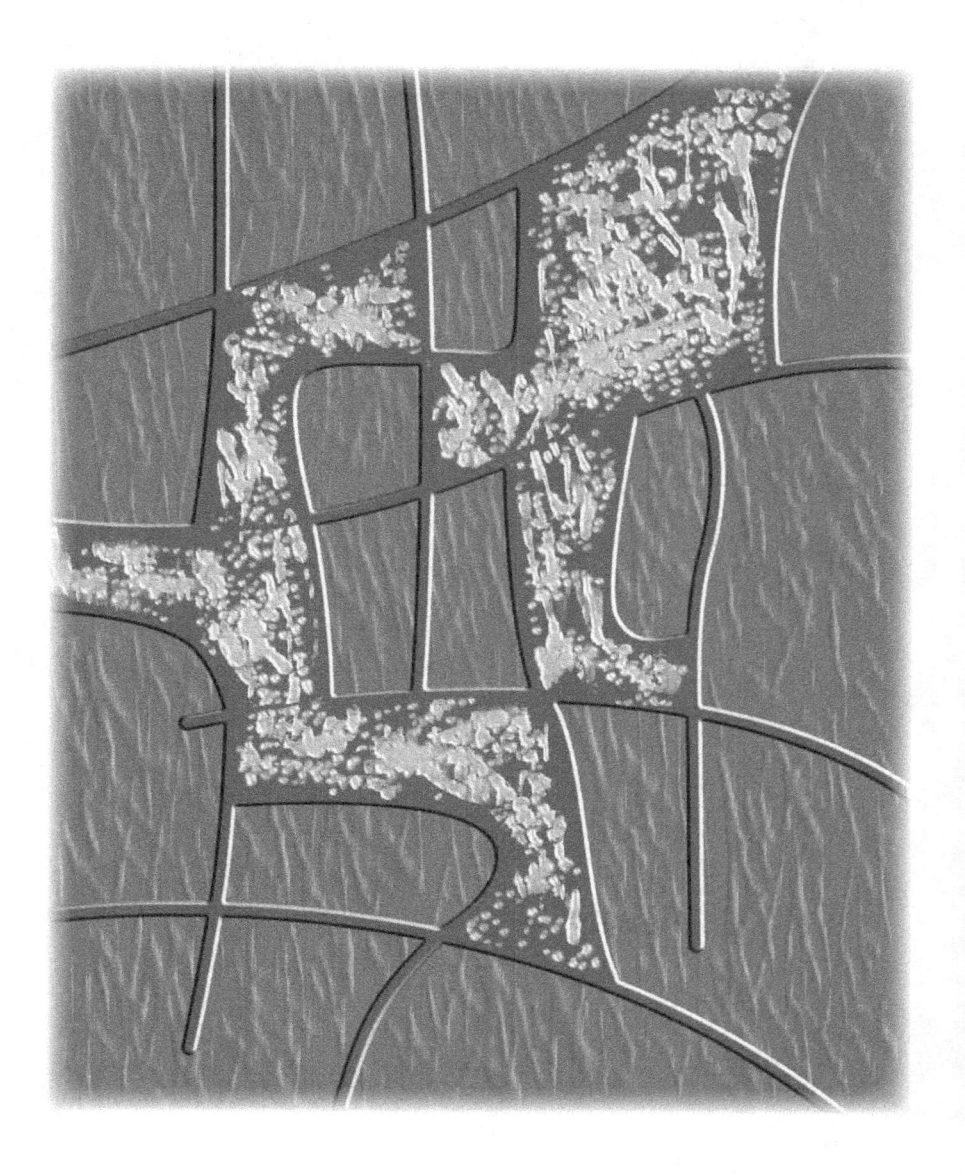

Chapter 2

Foreign Land

Whether flying or crawling, she still did not wish to think deeply about the issue because she doubted if she could understand the truth. A different happiness paved the way for a great curiosity that kept her senses wide open. It was a strange land; all around her eyes appeared things that could only be described with one word: beauty.

But the silence! She flinched. How strange it was; it had its own melody of sounds different from those she had known and heard on her planet. And the sounds throughout ensured, it could quite quickly drift pass pleasantly, unhindered. Strangeness or novelty? And the air, breathed so freely with ease. The air was not what she had felt before, but a gentle density of an unknown substance that stuck to every part of the body. This dense substance gradually encompassed her whole being but never restrained her free movement. Rather she was able to move much more freely and faster, like being assisted by someone who empowered her to perform, and did so with amusing grace and lightness. This air became lovelier, a friend without the desire to abandon her even for a second. Instead it helped her perform much better both inwardly and outwardly.

And again, upon closing her eyes, she noticed it was not exactly dark. The darkness was brighter than the brightness of the light she had known on Earth. If this was darkness, then what was this light doing here? She pondered over this bewilderment for a moment and then opened her eyes to peer curiously into the light. But she was surprised to notice endless, gentle and pastel softness in the coloured grey that surrounded the place.

In this grey light, black was just a shine that blinded her eyes, and she was not meant to resist its power, hence it was harmless. It appeared that this colour was attached somewhere around her, without being directly seen. Instead it was able to create colours and splendour in surrounding nature, which in turn made her become part of everything nearby. This invisible blackness was like a fabric in which every colour was absorbed by her and invariably became the same coloured stain, like the patterns of her features. Then she realized the people here looked quite different, unlike the people she was used to seeing in her permanent state on Earth.

Moreover, they had many different coloured paintings that changed every minute, whenever their thoughts changed or they shifted their gaze. Thus left them with the same human body and shape, but with their image printed as a coloured picture on their skin, which also changed according to the landscape and the objects upon which they were gazing.

They keep the same shape as a human body, but their image resembles a color imprint on their skin, ever-changing depending on the scenery that they are looking at and the image they are staring at, trying hard to harness all their thoughts.

She looked around, but there was nothing like water. It seemed ubiquitous, floating amongst everything, connecting and blending in unison in that unknown substance, which she inhaled with every breath like the air, though it enveloped it as if it were alive. Without any water to be seen, she felt something tangible somehow had dropped around her in small and large quantities, and she was relieved, her breathing and movement unimpeded.

All of that was just the beginning of building a normal life in this new land.

Chapter 3

Dreamed Trip

She shook deeply in all her senses and was encouraged to fight with confidence so as not to fail at her dreams in the race with difficulties and obstacles. Besides, uncertainty had disrupted her daily life and paved way for potentially unpleasant social encounters. She cried for conquering the cold windy peak, now drenched in beauty and delight. This achievement gave her inspiration.

Many days had gone by in her dreaming and waking up. She wondered about matters that worried her mind, and this raised a question mark while on her way to the other land. Of course she remembered the kiss, but how the rest of the journey happened was incomprehensible. Remembering every feeling, she was obliviously far from reality. She cherished every urge she had and every sight her eyes embraced. What was in that kiss that made her travel to a foreign land? Allowing herself the kiss had perhaps given her expectations of what was happening on another planet. Here the road was wide around the sunlit field, which was variegated from broken shadows of clouds and distant snowy mountains. And the weather was clear; this enabled her to enjoy the sights, which were revealed to her while travelling alone. She was obsessed by a desire to move forward while enjoying this new experience. She was travelling alone in something that resembled a car. It even looked like her car from the inside and she was completely compelled by a desire to continue ahead down the road that snakes (its way) through, far and wide in front of her, enthralled by this new experience. She didn't want to back away from the journey before reaching the peak, though knew there were still plenties of winds ahead.

The moment she approached the mountain, the weather became colder and cloudy. All of a sudden the whole car was engulfed by fog and then spit back out onto the sunlit path. These pictures of fog and sun changed more and more often. As she fell into this misty weather, she was confronted with a mind-boggling hesitation. And in this moment, she tried to spiritualize her imagination while at the same time she grappled with questions. Was the trip worth for the risk, and if she could ever reach the top, would there be something important or even interesting to see?

Only faith and confidence in the trustworthiness of the idea put the motivation into her. She suspected that she would enjoy it with a sense of pride, the lovely view from the top. Refusing to yield to pressure, even when thing seemed impenetrable. She saw this as a belief neither based on logical proof nor material evidence, as it might be on the ground.

As she reached the peak, which was lit by the sun like she had imagined, everything below was still groveling in fog. And the wind kept blowing, though not strongly, only to remind her that the summit was always windy. This peak was more or less like a victory over her irrational beliefs and she was now rewarded by faith, which had given her confidence when the path was almost invisible. Empowered by hope, she then determined to move along further despite the discouraging factors around and feelings of doubts that had seized her entire being.

Upon reaching the top, she was confused and surprised after seeing its geographic makeup. She realized it was a foreign land that looked similar to her own Earth but dynamically brimmed with many observable different colours. An unknown land with the same structure as the Earth, where everything seemed familiar? This portrayed a very tremendous phenotypic shift across the landscapes.

Satisfied with her own enthusiasm, she felt the need to return home. But the way which she presumed would take her back home instead led her elsewhere. All the streets and houses had striking similarities to her hometown, making it simple enough to navigate. But odd variations made her eventually realize that she had come into a new and an unfamiliar city quite different from hers, with tremendous phenotypic diversity across its geographically distributed populations.

She landed into an unknown home, but curiosity gingered up the quest to play as an August visitor.

Otherland

Chapter 4

On a Visit

The moment she entered the house, she was pretty sure it was not hers, but surprised to know it belonged to the same boy she had previously met and allowed herself to be kissed. And again to realize that many people seemed to have been informed about her arrival, as if they were expecting to see a close relative. It was a warm welcome of great astonishment, and she realized that the boy had already talked much about her.

She still couldn't understand how it had happened to be fallen into such an unknown world where he came from. Although in their first meeting, while she asked him where he came from, she expected to hear the name of a city, without assuming the answer to be a kiss that brought such unimaginable contents.

As a gesture of courtesy, a kind woman who stood before her took her gently by the hand and led her away from the other guests who watched her curiously while smiling. They walked down a long corridor decorated with pictures which she admired with curiosity and amusement. The corridor was filled with the smell of flowers, well arranged in the corners near the floor. Getting closer to the door, she hoped to come into another room, but instead found herself outside, where it was finely snowing. But there was no time to enjoy this winter wonderland. They walked down a path that led them into a small room where they found themselves alone, close to a warm fire and a large wooden table filled with delicious food. But an aromatic scent from brewing tea was enough to fascinate her and therefore left no room for any desire for food.

It was unclear: either the woman had wanted to heal the wounds that the girl had forgotten or the girl had wanted to talk about her failures and doubt which still hampered her happiness. Both had the need to talk. The woman was so caring, like a grandmother talking to her granddaughter. They held each other's hands and in the older woman's eyes there was an expression of warmth. This made the girl start thinking how nice and purifying staying here might be, like it was an action designed to bring people together.

Upon returning to the guestroom where the entertainment was still going on, she started dancing and at the same tried getting acquainted with some of the invited relatives and friends. She had dressed very simply, yet her clothes showed the great curves of her body. And she danced mostly with the boy. He basically introduced her to everyone who danced with them. The drinks were refreshing and intoxicating, making them talk and dance more.

Eventually, one after the other, everyone became tired and started leaving empty while others went to their respective rooms to sleep.

The boy struck up a somewhat romantic conversation with her, as if trying to keep the girl a little bit longer. But they talked until sleep took her away from him.

Dide

Otherland

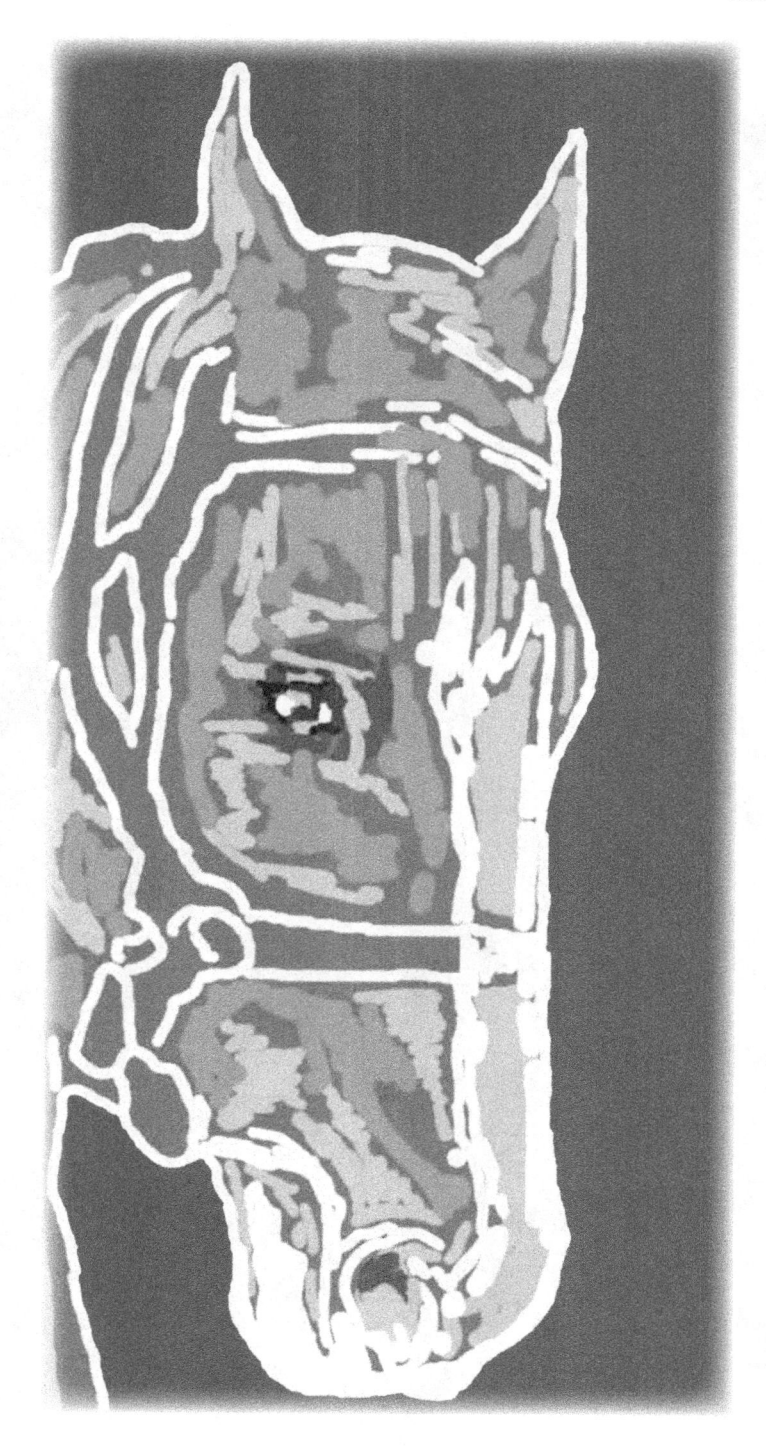

Chapter 5

Unwound Yarn

A long thread unwound over the stairs as he passed through the door. He almost touched the bed where she lay awake and covered with a warm blanket, enjoying a sweet odour from baking cookies. The windows were mostly covered with snow. There was a public holiday which children and adults were enjoying; this only made them pay more attention to one other in such a specific way unlike ordinary days.

Last night the boy had unwound a small loop of thread in her dress. He held the end of this thread when she went upstairs to sleep. The loop became more and more unwound until it went out of her reach and caused the chaos of yarn in her room. As she bustled, her room became a net of unwound thread and the dress unravelled. When she saw the chaos she smiled, because among the mess of unwound thread was a hidden thought of happiness that, at the other end of the thread, was the one that was the reason for her to stand stark naked before herself.

While she was getting away from him, she failed to hide away from herself, thinking about her truths and lies. Though he hadn't seen her, he knew that she was naked, telling everything about herself and getting to understand her own story. He hadn't heard the contents of that story, but irrespectively, he felt happy that he was the reason for her looking deep into her own self. At this moment she assumed that the boy was expecting her now with deep curiosity to see if the new garment would perhaps leave an eye-popping impression. All these thoughts flashed through her head while she contemplated about what to wear. Though there was no option that didn't start with difficult, in reality it was less important because her clothes were like others. In this land, everyone dressed with clothes strictly made with different styles based on individual taste. The same was her wardrobe, full of clothes especially for her. Besides, she was a bit confused last night probably because of her thoughts about him.

As she went down the stairs, happiness took hold of her because of the thoughts that the thread-unravelling had put in her. Upon seeing her, his smile was frank and wide, his face radiant. Though no one had talked about the unravelled dress which made her to believe, many different people might have many different points of view which often ridged their characteristics to reason from circumstance. The day encouraged them to talk about their lovely breakfast, her warm tea and his fragrant coffee.

Meanwhile, the sun penetrating the window vents prompted her to go out into the garden. She noticed him behind her. And as he got closer, he whispered how beautiful she looked. His voice was soft and dense. Every single word that rolled out of his beautifully shaped lips was clear and easy to understand. She felt the warmth of his skin as he got closer. He took a little radio from his pocket, and began to change the stations, looking inquiringly at her and pondered what kind of song she would like to listen. Then he smiled, his face was putting up emotional expression while the eyes were at the same time showing all the goodness of the world from the gift of his amazing tenderness. She started to lose herself in his presence, but he knew how to take good care of her, even better than she could. And this made her to see herself being at the most secured place in the world. Her confidence in him made her less worried about any danger.

His care was so beautiful. He would never sit down first; he would make sure that she was seated comfortably where she had chosen to sit before sitting down himself. Everything that was on her mind was important to him. Everything she thought of, everything she intended to do, as well as every choice of hers. He would never oppose her. He would be interested in everything she was interested in instead. That made his opinions even more important to her and she would always take it into consideration.

His hands were big and strong and he reached out when she stumbled while walking and listening to the music. His body radiated power that made him look even bigger. But the chest in which his good heart beat seemed wrapped with velvet skin, concealing every muscle and vein. But there was no ostentation in his behaviour, and suddenly she wanted to show him to the world where she belonged, because her eyes loved him and now her heart had become a home for his soul.

Baffled with these thoughts, she decided to lean on one of the trees and noticed the blossoms were not only on the branches but also now covering her hair. He put his fingers into her hair, gently removing every flower. After taking the last one, he shrank his fingers in such a playful manner indicating, he held nothing neither. This gesture however attracted her gaze towards the four fingers, which were revolving in front of her face.

Afterward, he held out his hand, and it was empty save for his warmth.

His fingers were all she was seeing at that moment.

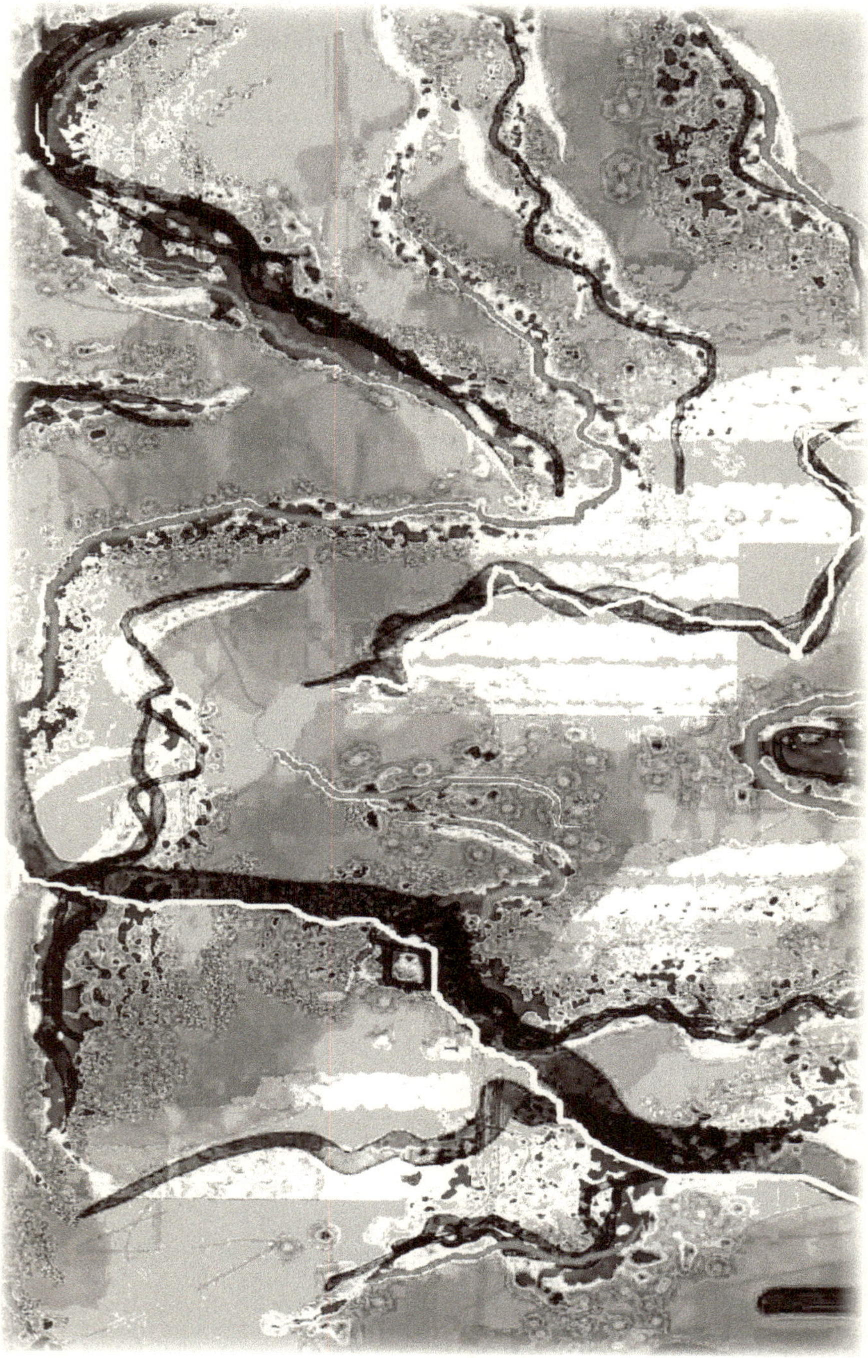

Chapter 6

Those Fingers

This fist of four fingers which obviously were holding nothing inside, were hiding the warmth they had attracted her with. She approached them filled with a desire to make sure nothing escaped her glance. Nothing was hidden in the clench of these beautiful, strong fingers. All the strength was in the fingers themselves. She was longing to uncover the truth that mesmerized her.

Now she was enchanted, somehow unlike the girl who had relaxed against the blossoming tree. She seemed to have transformed into small particles, thanks to those fingers.

She was no longer the girl, leaning against the blossoming tree, but an infinitely tiny particle, which got lost in the four fingers where she followed every move they made.

She felt their secrets when they moved on her body, but doubted if eye-tracking alone could on its own provide enough confidence to master their movements. Over the course of time, patterns emerged from their movements which revealed their occasional hidden agendas. She saw his fingers as part of that great body, the one which had shown her things that were previously incomprehensible. Then she would understand what had happened to her before, this time through the eye of a tiny particle. This particle was part of the big united body, which had gone through all those things that had in the past remained invisible to it and had aroused questions about small details that had remained impossible to understand. She began to realize that the difference between people was the freedom to experience and express things in different ways. Treating the same story with different understandings and knowing that the same event could play different roles in the lives of people that occupied different environments, occupying a different space in their souls and having a different impact on the following circumstances in their daily lives. As those little blossoms wandered into the space between his fingers, she recognized the differences between people and their contradictions. She was moved and obsessed by these wonders which exist not only on the planet but also within its inhabitants, as well as intrigued by the secret hidden between those fingers.

The girl was that tiny particle in a foreign land, hidden between the boy's fingers. It was there that she found her answers to all the questions and she would often reminisce about them after that.

One of the questions that had remained in her was about people's feelings and the persistence of their faith reflected in peace and love that filled people's hearts. Things that had perplexed her before, now gave birth to her amazement at the feelings those answers stirred.

This however brought the answer to one of her questions which would be asked afterward. But still, another question remained unanswered, stubbornness and anger of people when they said they love. She felt that love was a willingness to sacrifice for others' happiness. And this made her convinced, people had never felt love in the same manner in which it was been spoken. Things which had astonished her before now gave her the feeling of amusement.

Nevertheless, some places on Earth were filled with hatred and riots, but in spite of all these barriers, people still managed to live in peace with great kindness and love for one another.

There have been innumerous instances when helpless and hopeless people have overwhelmed the impossible, performing a seemingly miraculous feat, persistent in the only faith which have fostered their last hope of deliverance in critical situations. Then again, how many more in possession of considerable privileges and enjoying riches few others would ever touch, squander that wealth of opportunity without ever succeeding to add something to it and build their own happiness which would bring them joy?

Such people sink in the abyss of their own pernicious destruction without any gratitude for the happiness that already belongs to them and for which they didn't have to put their faith to the test not because they are holding it in their hands, but because of their lack of faith they lost what they already have.

There are many places on Earth, riddled with riots and calamities, but despite the teeming problems, even in these hot spots there are people who live with peace in their hearts and who are ready to offer mercy and tender care to their neighbour.

In many other peaceful places in the world, where comfort and affluence provide safety and peace, but irrespective of this there are people living there that are ravaged with malice and envy, vengefulness and aggression; they hate love for everything and for all. These fates, controversial beliefs and events that contradict circumstances, are all equally real as part of life. Since, when accepted in different ways life, it can be controversial, absurd or a miracle which is lived every day, but more than anything else, life varies in its nature.

Although these sensations were larger than all the knowledge she had had when she was the girl leaning against the blossoming tree, she now managed to hold this huge pile of feelings in herself, as the small particle she had become.

After a while she turned into the girl leaning against the blossoming tree again and the boy next to her buried his fingers in her hair.

She looked at him with understanding eyes and it seemed as if she was now seeing his world more clearly.

He embraced her and they left.

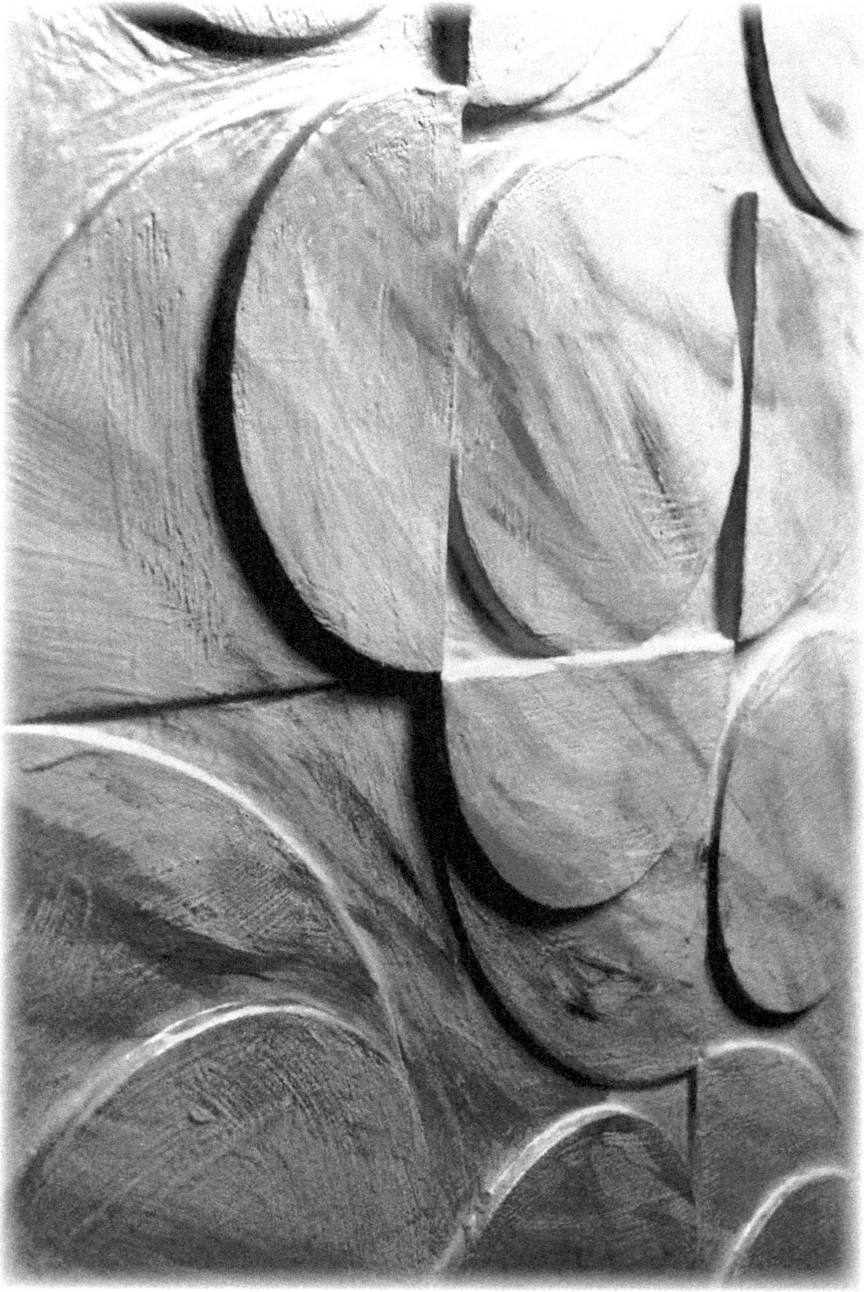

Chapter 7

Pleasant Walking

The whole afternoon was perfect. He wished to show her everything, and to especially things which were so precious to him. They walked down streets that shone like glass overrun with water. But there was no water here; the people absorbed it from the air and each could absorb as much as the body needed. There were flourishing trees alongside the streets and lots of greenery around the buildings as well. Instead of natural water on its chemical form, there was hot viscous liquid that provides year-round hydrant to the street, keeping them easier to clean, dry and far from freezing.

However, the same fluids were used for heating local homes. But instead of pipes, these fluids were connected into a single hole, from there, it passed through the streets to reach each home.

Every house was built with transparent flat roofs, to serve as playgrounds for children. There were no swimming pools; instead children love to play with the powdery sand, made up of jelly pellets that could be easily compressed and flattened, the better to build with.

These small balls had the strange feature of looking like powder at ease, but they would immediately turn to jelly once touched, thus providing children with the opportunity to construct. But, once it was no longer touched, the substance turned into powder again. That's why all the towers and castles looked as if they had been powdered.

Taxis were different, too. Instead of having four wheels, they were known as Big Balls. People entered and the ball rolled, making the movements easier and faster. The same jelly-like substance was used to manufacture these vehicles. What seemed like jelly at first sight and of what all their vehicles were made, was not the same matter that kids used to build the castles. The substance was hard like a diamond but looked like a jelly. Though there was no provision to call taxis, people walked to the taxi stand where various colourful balls were parked. After choosing the colour they preferred by inserting a coin in a lateral hole, the ball opened and they rolled. Inside a Big Ball, one could sit comfortably. One had to specify his destination in other to facilitate the Big Ball navigation system.

Despite the outer coloured layer of the ball, from the inside everything looked transparent, revealing the whole scenery outside.

The boy explained about some of the attractions alongside the street. She was impressed by the beauty and variety of towers that scattered the streets. Each of these symbolized one event, person or advertisement. Inside them were public libraries. He told her that on this planet, people like to read using not only contemporary media, but also books which unfold page by page, like on Earth. But their books were made of a thin plastic material, derived from household waste products. He carefully pulled a book from his bag like it was his favourite. Here people were concerned so much about books and this made them handle them with great care, love and attention. He opened it to demonstrate to her how interesting reading it would be, once it was opened. From the book came light, not shining in her eyes but illuminating and making the text easily readable. To them reading was a loving pursuit, so these libraries were constantly filled with people of all ages and all walks of life, who occasionally went to read with pleasure there.

Moreover, this had brought a living image to the town due to its strange shapes and colourful patterns of the towers, thus turning them into real paintings and sculptures. Industries as well as administrative buildings were clustered at one place, close to one end of the town and surrounded by transparent covers that projected greenery around them.

Dide

Thus the main image of every town or village consisted mainly of houses, a lot of greenery around them and a tiny area covered by a see-through dome.

There were also places for entertainment, mostly in the open because here people met to have fun or to rest outside. Clubs, cinema theaters and entertainment centers were outdoors and when the weather got worse or it's raining, they were covered by a see-through dome, similar to that of the administrative buildings.

The Big Ball in which they were being driven pulled over in front of a restaurant located at one end of the park with a large meadow and a few alleys. As they sat down, the boy asked for the menu traditionally meant for this restaurant. On that were honeydew, salad, rolled dough and juice. While eating they talked about the food and the nature of the service. There was no water; instead juices with dense nectars or jelly creams were served.

After they finished eating, they decided to walk to a rink, where they played a ball game with rules, which he explained very well, and later they drove back home.

The boy lived alone. The guests had left and his parents lived a few blocks away. So when they were going home, they were on their own. He accompanied her to her room, leaving her alone to get ready for bed.

Otherland

Chapter 8

Awake while in Love

In her sleep, she dreamt she had a crush on him, while her love was only just beginning to blossom. And his voice quietly brought her to excitement. To her, words were not enough to be used to express or compare her feelings for him. She believed they were parts of this feeling, which was so calm, inclusive and made them to feel belonging. Neither wished to go away from where they were.

They were happy and this happiness they shared had given way to sweetness, which made them enjoy everything that happened around them.

She started falling for him in her dream.

Whatever great truth is revealed, it cannot compare with the words that choose love and that are an intrinsic part of it. Such words are calm, they feel at home, that's why they don't need to run away and they want to be exactly where they are. They are happy with the happiness they have and they are not looking for anything else. They enjoy everything that is happening at this very moment. Even a lie cannot muffle or change such calm words, because the words of the lie, unbearable by nature, restlessly try to escape their own presence and no matter whether the place is a nice or a nasty one, they will leave. Only warmth can stay, if it has existed at one point, because it does not run cold irrespective of the cold that will pass through it. Warmth always chooses love, feeling confident in it and if it moves away, it loses itself and it turns into anything else, but not warmth born of love.

Saying words with warmth, we choose to love. Such were her words and they made her warm and filled her with love that remained lingering in her heart even after she was wide awake. You might be clumsy, but you can do it. So it goes, when you are in love. Imperfection is no obstacle or impediment for you. It may make your actions look foolish and funny. However, you die to do these things, believing that these imperfect acts get you closer to the perfection of love.

She was dreaming how awkwardly she was moving next to him, possessed with the controversies and confusion, stirred by love with which he wrapped her and which crawled into her soul. His actions were a bit controversial, because longing to do something that would please her, he turned ordinary gestures into complicated and confused actions. This baffled her a bit and, when it happened unexpectedly, it even startled her. He turned even the simple act of giving her a flower into something complicated. In his desire to be original and unique, he chose a flower which was actually a huge white fluffy puff, so light and bigger than her in size and with a tiny brown stick instead of a stalk. When she hugged her present, this puff-shaped flower (which resembled candy floss) turned out that its white matter sticky and it all stuck all over her. At first, she was terrified, then she was bemused and then she started laughing, after she saw embarrassed boy who was fidgeting around her, trying to unglue his present.

He later accompanied her to a children's playground where he took some jelly like substance and covered her body. To her, this was inappropriate because of the sticky nature of the substance. However, she started smiling after discovering it was easy to remove. As all this was going on, suddenly she awoke and didn't remember exactly what she had dreamt about.

But she enjoyed the feelings that the dream had left in her. However, she failed to understand whether it was selfishness or generosity that played this role in her dream. Instead she believed it was much easier to love than to hate.

So she became confused, not knowing what to expect. She acknowledged that her world was not physically pure. She did not understand how such anguish could manifest into her life or how such could be changed when she got tired of everything around her. She was living in despair and pain, rather than embracing hope, love and happiness. The world was full of dreams and quests for adventures.

Embracing this change was vital because progress would appear impossible without this. And those who cannot change their minds cannot change anything.

Many things did not exist before, but all appeared to be happening now. She was so much in love until she had this dream in this unknown planet which revealed the happiness and beauty she was searching for. And there were no answers to all her questions.

But all that she could not find in the answers to those questions of hers, but in the new adventures that she was experiencing in this new land.

Otherland

Chapter 9

Flying Device

She wanted to be happy and it happened when she realized only when she was standing alone and calm with herself, at peace with herself, finding so many small things that she now knew deserved her smile. She was happy finding out that the world was a nicer and more comfortable place to live in than before, because before she was looking at it through different eyes. She felt stronger and more confident, realizing that she was holding her dreams in her hands. Her happiness depended on her alone and she possessed everything to make it happen. It was wonderful to feel powerful and at the same time at peace in the quiet of her solitude, where she began to understand and love the world around her more and more, as well as life itself, which she inhaled like a gift with every breath she took and which turned her into a wonderful and happy person.

She sat alone on a high rock where she had waited for him to come back from collecting some dry leaves and branches for a fire. As she waited, her attention was captivated by the beauty of the place, which revealed so much about the height of the rock. From that moment, she became aware of the difference in nature in the land where he came from.

The forest here had the same blue-green colour as the ocean. And the wind moved trees like the movement of algae inside the water. The leaves were deep blue to pale green and refracted light. When the birds flew, their movements were fish-like and their songs were like when dolphins cried. The rocks were the same, but soft and smooth when touched, as if covered with velvet and satin.

The boy brought along with him on his way back some pieces of clay and amber. Apparently it was not possible to light a fire with dry twigs, but with resin, which could be found only in the trunks of trees. Here in the land, people loved "going green" by planting many new trees in the forest. The boy put the resin down on the ground, took out a small white piece of cloth from his pocket and when he rubbed the resin with it small cones started forming slowly and growing with their points upwards. These cones formed and multiplied along the whole surface of the resin. The fire looked hard and transparent like icicles, gradually rising from the earth to reach a certain height and then break by only to begin to grow again. To stop the fire from burning he broke off more from the same white piece. Then he threw away the broken pieces that formed cones in other to stop them from burning. The leftover fire was used for fuel to facilitate his mountain glider.

This flying device was a machine built with a cylinder engine, very light and easy to carry in a backpack. It had long strips of cloth on its two ends. It was made of shiny fabric, sewn together with fabric sleeves that fitted into same backpack. In flight they became air tubes, curved like a rainbow over the cylinder where they sat. This cylinder engine was large enough to accommodate two of them. After assemblage, they sat on it and flew to a high cliff. This gave them an incredible feeling of excitement.

In flight, people could understand each other better. Many people loved to talk while flying, because they enjoyed the same feeling while viewing an incredible and sensational movement of this device in the air. They also used this opportunity to settle their differences among themselves. She was moved by this new system of communication. It was so unlike people on Earth who quarrelled nervously about things such as noise, poverty, lack of basic amenities, spiritual anguish, life experiences in different social environments, and over ambition. They couldn't understand the meaning of the same words with the same sense as others.

During this flight though, people shared everything in common, ranging from food, drinks and whatever.

While they were flying on that planet, they forgot about their past, forgiving themselves and all the others everything and thus isolating themselves in a peaceful environment, away from previous distractions and irritants, sharing the same conditions of life. Those people started building their own new perceptions, equally understandable and having the same meaning for all of them, leaving only the difference in strength of these words. But the very meaning of the word became the same and in this way, the perception of differences they had argued before became the same.

The conflict between people is like when two paupers have to share one coin. With this one and only coin they could buy a loaf of bread and a bottle of water, which they would again have to share. But, if one of the paupers had eaten only salted fish for the previous couple of days, he would be dying of thirst, whereas the other had been drinking only water, would be starving. Then they would incessantly be arguing—the hungry one craving for bread and the thirsty one longing for water. They would probably die while arguing, because neither would allow the other to decide.

But imagine the same paupers living for a week together, sharing food and water, residing in a place where there was no shortage of food and water, which they share together in their closely-knit community. Imagine now giving those people a coin again and a chance to choose what to buy: food or water. They would make an unanimous choice immediately, depending on whether they feel more hungry or thirsty. The same thing happened during the flights on the boy's planet, as if while the people there were flying they were eating and drinking while sharing common goods, being in the same environment and all that smoothed their differences.

She was really obsessed by the system, and then saw him as someone very dear to her. The area was so high and viewable like from a peak of a mountain, where deer and a few small animals were seen in the meadows and the birds seen carelessly flying and singing merrily.

The boy landed the glider in a meadow filled with pink flowers, which they gathered into a large bouquet. Then they continued with their walk, along the forest path that led them to a hut where they stopped to spend the night, planning to have another walk the next day before rolling back home in the Big Ball.

Otherland

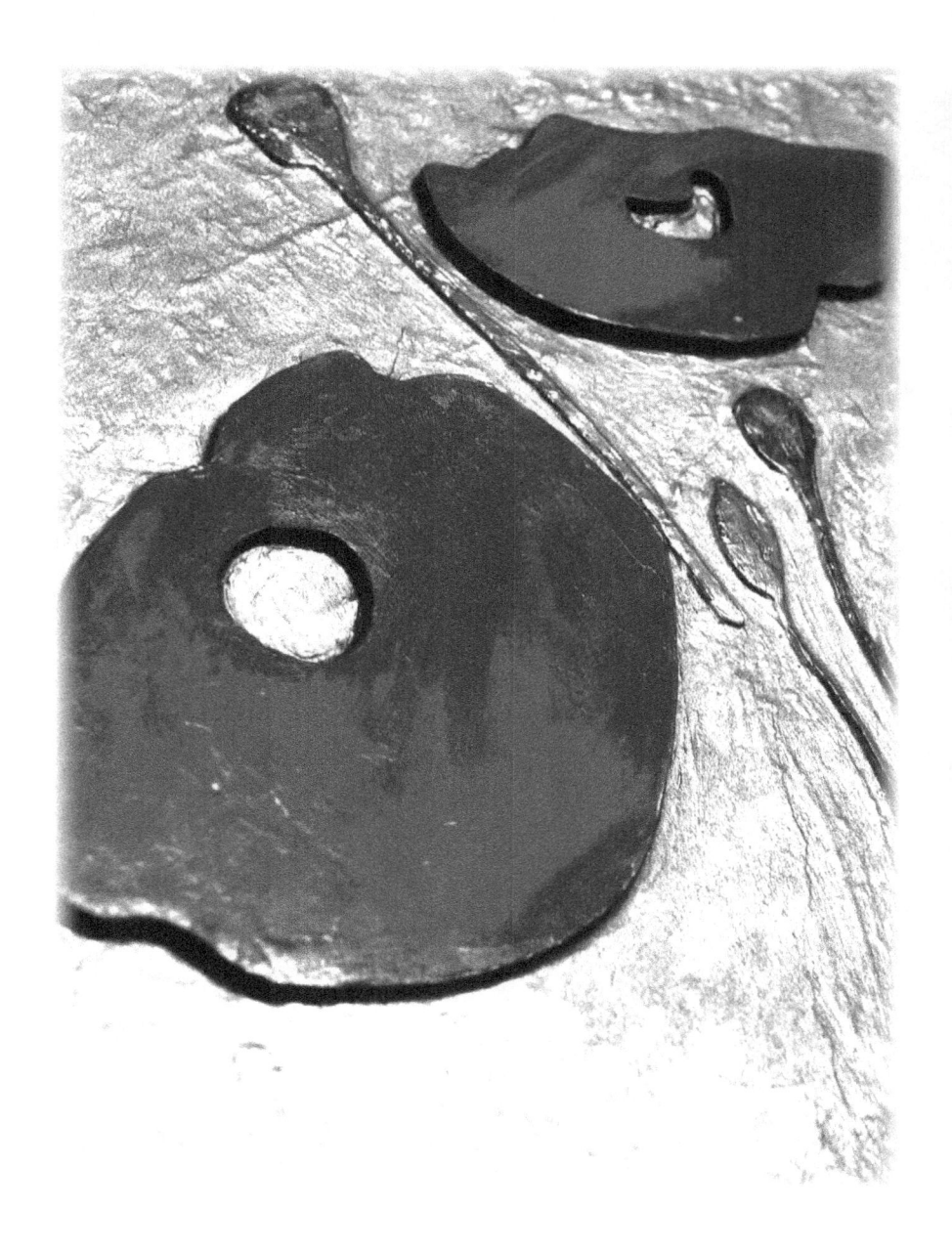

Chapter 10

Fluctuating Clouds

They had planned to sleep in a planetarium that could accommodate many people. Here, people slept in sleeping bags on warm heated floors beneath a transparent rooftop, making it possible for one to view the starry sky from inside. And they were served hot soup, vegetable sauce and roasted sweet apples on the balcony before going to sleep. So after a brief conversation with other visitors of this hut, they now went to their various sleeping places where most of them had already fallen asleep.

He slipped into his bag next to her and whispered goodnight. Everywhere was quiet and she could hear his breathing. As she turned over to sleep, the glass that was revealing the beauty and nature of the surrounding place captured her interest and brought her focus upward. She hoped to capture every moment and every movement of the stars as well as to explore their magnificence and brilliance. To her, having all these views was more important than sleep. After seeing their performances in the sky, she felt as though she was in the starry theatre, where stars were the actors. The stars were really moving as if they were going on a mission and very much in a hurry. Music was not so audible but like a whisper and reminiscent of songs her mother had always sung to her when she was a little child.

The story of the repeated mistakes was being told. Everything was happening before her eyes and all the emotions reminded her of previous mistakes and disappointments that were so painful. These memories appeared and disappeared. The story the stars were telling made her remember mistakes she had regretted. But presently, she regretted nothing.

Her heart was free, knowing where to take her and what to do. She realized that, more than anything else, she wanted never to lose this joy which was born in her. She was aware that this joy existed in her and was interested only in that to make the person next to her feel loved. She wanted to meet people with the only purpose to share her love and thus making them happy.

Meanwhile, the night made her days full of happiness and paved the way for new sensational feelings quite different from the remorse that plagued her past. In this starry theatre, lying comfortably inside her sleeping bag, she was moved by how the stars sang without hesitation. They seemed to be singing a song that was so compassionate and pure that gave voice to the voiceless, making them stand against all odds.

The story of the stars that they played echoed in the days of her life, but this echo was not filled with pity and pain, but twisted gently past every thought of hers and every flutter, turning it into a love song. This song enchanted her, coming deep from the open and sincere soul of a man in love who sings for his beloved that is far away from him, living in doubt whether he really loved her or not. This song was sad and sorrowful, but also cleansing. The melody slowly turned into a gentle whining of the wind that brought the warm voices of determined boldness, which calmly overcomes all obstacles and difficulties and without arguing keeps going forward.

Soon the tune became quiet. Finally, when each star was bowing down like an actor about to display its role, the song became lovelier and seemed to come from a butterfly that wants to sip on sweet nectars. The song spread ethereally, making everything around a part of this spectacle. All this was going on throughout the night and she did not miss anything, thus forgetting about her sleep.

Once the sun had started to appear on the horizon, the curtains of this event started to close with the whiteness of coming dawn. Then, she remembered another song by the sun, smiling on Earth and never wished to stop to rise despite fluctuating clouds. It could only be hidden for sometimes, but never stopped to share its grace with Earth. Just to stay behind the clouds until they got tired, then allowed the Earth to be illuminated again. She was moved by this solar song until her eyelids began to close, carrying her off to her morning nap.

Otherland

Chapter 11

Wonderful Child

After waking up at noon, she realized others had woken up hours ago. Upon looking above, her gaze was captured by different colours of the clouds. This time around there were flying beetles, which glowed different colours of lights. She eagerly went outside to satisfy her curiosity. The movements of these luminous beetles led her to the foliage of a nearby meadow, where she saw an endless stream surrounded by incredible vegetation.

Her eyes were overwhelmed with joy. The stream appeared like colourless lava streaming downward on its runway. Astonished by the vegetation, she was confused about where to look next. But she was not seeking to discover the most beautiful place, rather to allow her eyes to crawl everywhere. So it would be enough to choose and to be consistent about it; perhaps her choice might be right.

Variety was confusing.

As she pondered, a child appeared from nowhere. The child took her by the hand with the desire to show her all the creatures of the planet. She followed in the child's footsteps, determined to see everything.

Her little guide was consistent. The decisions about what to watch as well as in which direction to focus her gaze belonged to the child. Her obligation was to follow and merely to trust her. However, the child showed a satisfactory feeling after seeing how amazed she was, about everything shown to her.

Somehow, this child taught her how to find her way whenever she got puzzled by decisions. This showed her how to follow a sequence without wasting any moment in doubts. Actually, she was following the nature of creativity and was organizing her focus from the directives given by the arm of the little child.

She thought about how adults were the children of the past and our children were the future and our happiness for tomorrow. While she was lost in thought, the little child plucked at her sleeve earnestly to show her new things. But suddenly she realized the boy might be waiting for her in the cabin and must feel somewhat embarrassed by her absence already.

She hurried back to him.

She told him about the pleasant walk with the unknown child. He smiled and said that people here more than anything else arranged their thoughts first, because it ensured their success. They never wished to waste their energy and forces in vain by struggling with random thoughts. This saying brought a flashback: how many times she had tried in vain to deal with common tasks, but the chaotic nature of her disordered thoughts confused and baffled her, thereby thwarting every effort.

Meanwhile, he wished to show her some animals they kept as pets: blue sheep with green stripes and orange cows with white spots, from which they extracted milk and wool. She saw many cute hens, all white with golden heads and light brown. And their eggs came with gold shells while inside were white yolks.

Dogs were graceful with elongated legs and smooth coats of various colours. One could also see different varieties of cats with green eyes and gray hair. These animals entertained visitors, who voluntarily assisted in caring for them. It made the animals very friendly and fond of every stranger.

Slowly the weather started to change with the approach of evening and they took their backpacks, hired a taxi and rolled back home.

Dide

Otherland

Chapter 12

Celebration

His relatives and friends had gathered again to celebrate another holiday. The house was full to capacity; they talked and laughed and used the opportunity to settle minor disputes. They also walked around the garden, where they engaged played games not meant for adults alone but children too. And they later regrouped inside the house to continue their talking and everyone felt welcome.

At one end of the garden was a unique plant, basically a huge tree with a thick trunk and large bumps to make it easier to climb. On its branches, instead of leaves were long pods filled with small balls. The branches shook from time to time, and during this process collided with one another, which resulted in creating a special type of noise that motivated everyone to climb. This plant stood in huge area solely covered with mud, full of pearly scales glittered in the sun.

Children liked to jump down from this tree to mud wrestle. But adults preferred always to slide. Some threw mud balls. Others stood and amused themselves by watching the show. The glittering particles were so useful for the skin; they were enriched with certain vitamins needed for health. People engaged in this game basically for its healthy purposes and whenever they became tired of being muddy, they would retreat.

Besides this muddy area of the garden, there was another with trees and flowers as well as grasses. And other part known as a straw kingdom, noted for its long and dry golden grasses, soft like cotton, which children loved to twist in the process of hiding or which they used to make fluffy pillows on which to jump.

No one was ever upset at anyone!

It was a golden rule that a girl has to learn from one of the guests who practiced as a doctor. During the process everyone learned that the most important thing for human health was not to carry guilt or blame. The principle of health had taught them to never to blame others. They believed that in every situation, one has always a choice. They were able to make their wishes and to settle down with the belief that love would create circumstances which would allow life to be filled with events that would bring success and happiness.

Faith had made it easy for them to embrace courage and made their hearts strong and free and thus kept them in good health. The doctor worked more like a psychologist who rarely prescribed anything, but used other procedures like interviews conducted together combined with exercises performed in his presence. Health was treated purely with peace of mind. This peace was built on interpersonal relationships where anger, hatred and revenge were considered serious diseases and patient were cared for with warmth from their doctors and relatives.

Emotional comfort was a priority there. One of the requirements needed to be a local politician was to be of good health. Politicians were one of the happiest kinds of people because they were extremely compassionate. Therefore, soldiers and policemen were not many in number. There were many more people in aviation because it was used in all fields: transport, agriculture, science and emergencies. This profession was one of the favorites, not only among boys, but also among girls. The boy that brought her to this planet was also a pilot.

They had lawyers too, but legally they always worked together with accountants. In each law firm or suit, a lawyer and accountant were required to appear and exist together. This ensured a quick and fair resolution of outstanding disputes without any financial burden on either side.

Similarly, each bank functioned as an advisory firm, where citizens were consulted about all economic matters concerning them. Banks were called financial and economic bureaus. However, any financial and economic bureau was required to be connected to one politician. This made the number of politicians and banks in the country more or less equivalent. This system ensured more transparency as well as control over public finances.

According to the boy's cousin, who worked as a musician, every type of art, both music and otherwise, were united under one generic title of "artistic environment" and was directly linked under the law to the health system. Both health professionals and artists were provided by the State and citizens were freely allowed to visit doctors or concerts.

While the girl had been watching some of the family games, she managed to get acquainted with the relatives, who worked in different professions. She was a bit sad as she stood alone at one end of the garden, watching how others played. She started thinking about her own land and the laws that ruled over there. She was overwhelmed by homesickness.

But this quickly disappeared with one muddy ball thrown to her by him, bringing her back to the show.

As a matter of concern, the host knew in advance how long each guest would stay and when he was scheduled to leave; some came just for a few hours while others wanted to stay until late evening. Although it was natural, any departure caused sadness not only to the host, but also to those who wished to stay a little longer.

These people loved to be united. They cheered and grieved together. They lived separately but united, and divided but joined together. Every holiday began with smiles and ended with sadness, for fear of separation till the next possible event. She was part of this celebration, a truly loved and long-awaited guest, and she felt love and acceptance from them.

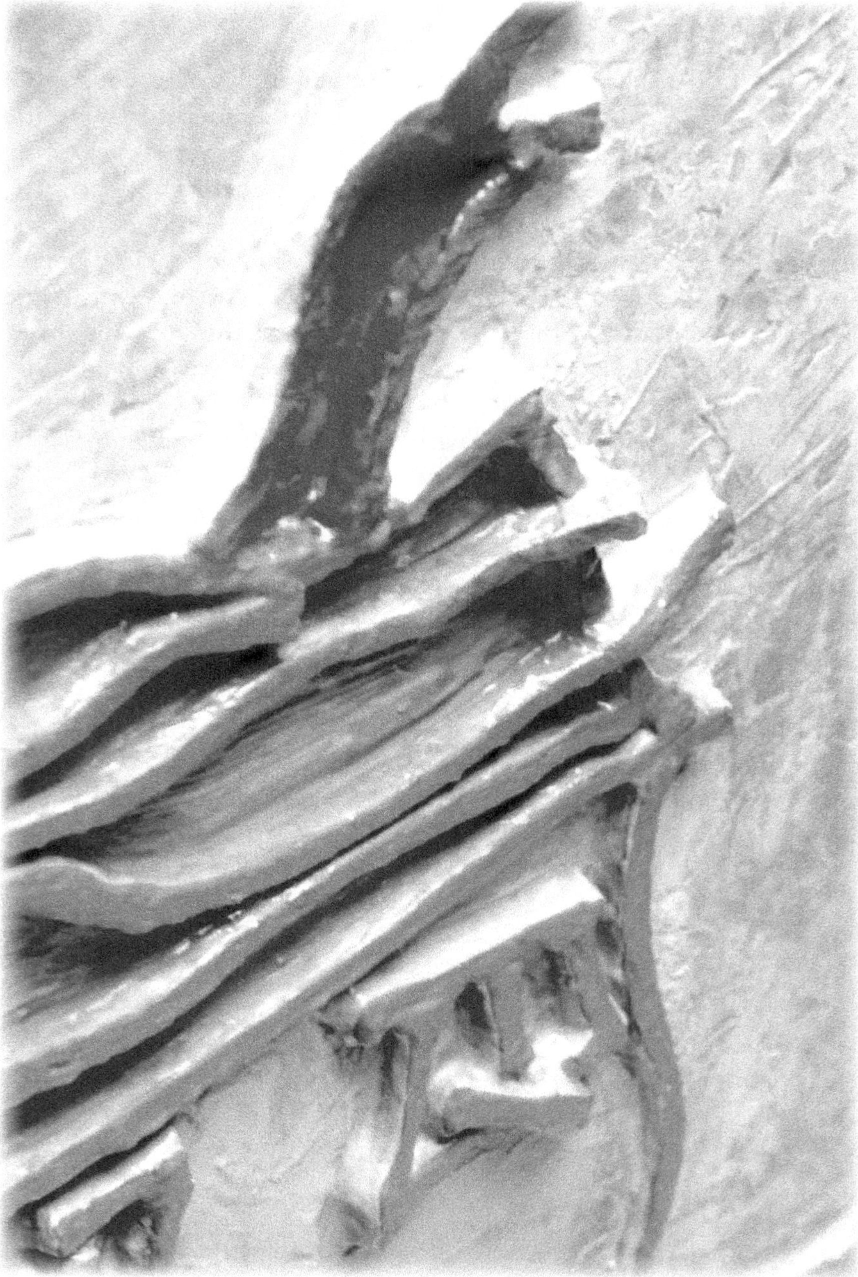

Chapter 13

Storm

The next day, while he helped his parents with the greenhouse, she was left alone for hours.

She decided to use the time to back him a whimsical cake from her mother's recipe, as a surprise for him. As she was putting necessary ingredients together, her attention was distracted by some harsh wind from the opened windows. She rushed to close the windows, but as she went to the door, there she noticed with great astonishment the wind was blowing without affecting the leaves or branches. This unprecedented development dumbfounded her, so she decided to go out to the garden.

Aware of the severe weather, she still decided to walk down to the meadow, which was not so far from the house. The trees stood unshaken and appeared as if the storm had no strength to move them. This made her rightfully focused much attention on the power behind that.

As she was trying to understand the way in which the storm raged, she started feeling its effect on her face, but not her hair. Her heart became paralyzed with horror but she did not see any sign of devastation. A couple of minutes later, she turned her gaze and noticed things had completely changed. It appeared these fundamental changes had happened behind her, while she was looking in another direction. She did not understand. How had those slender trees risen majestically a minute after she looked at them? There were broken branches, stems and uprooted trees, but without any sound of devastation. Everything seemed to be happening behind her, completely hidden from her sight.

As she ran around, she noticed some places were more damaged than others. She finally acknowledged this violent upheaval as a result of changes that occurred in everything around her. As she was plunged into chaos, she walked down to the river that looked so calm, but was flowing full of a transparent substance. Water sprayed all over her and hampered her breathing. She became increasingly exhausted, while struggling with all her strength to free herself from the water. But the happiness she felt was short lived.

She later found herself on the sand with sparse vegetation, illuminated by bright sunshine. But instead of feeling the heat, she felt the coldness of sharp blades from an invisible moving grass that cut her feet. She couldn't see the grass, but could feel the wounds on her ankles and feet.

At this juncture, she decided to sit beside a huge tree so as to energize herself, convinced that its leaves would protect her from the sun. Instead she became helpless after seeing her hair soaked from the rain, which dropped invisibly but could be seen and felt streaming downward on her face. She now saw herself at a crossroad, putting her head in between her knees she pressed strongly so as to make the horror echo and disappear.

And hours later, after waking up, her body could not remember how long she had slept or nothing about the storm. Still she dared not move.

She began slowly to rediscover some blissful feelings, sensing gradually the warmth of the sun as well as the fresh air. However, she managed to regain her sensitivity against anything which might come from somewhere to consolidate another resource for cataclysm. Still, her heart was broken and bruised from the confusing storm and she hurried home to the boy's house, shutting the door behind her.

Once there, she sat comfortably on a sofa, covered in a blanket and toying playfully with her cup of tea, which helped to recuperate her strength lost in the horrible episode.

She remembered the cake she had started, and deemed it worthwhile to continue with the preparation. This involvement in a household activity brought about feelings of belonging and usefulness.

Dide

Her beloved boy later came back with his parents. His appearance took away all her fears and horrifying memories. Now the world looked different because she was at home, where she felt loved and was engaged in pretty pursuits, like baking a cake and dining together.

Otherland

Chapter 14

Flames of Joy

It was yet another morning in this wonderful and unknown country. The light in the room was brighter than on the outside. She snuggled in the fluffy cover as she loved to do so many mornings.

As she was still lying on her bed, she saw the world that had begun in her room and stretched beyond her thoughts. The challenges of the day were so pressing and appalling, and other daily activities yet undone. After taking her breakfast she has to meet with the boy, who had gone out earlier for a jog in a nearby park. She said she would meet him and bring along his little bag in which there were some things he needed.

They had an arrangement: She was supposed to find him in the park and bring him his small bag with the details, which he needed to exchange in the store that they were to visit together. After taking the bag, she left for the park. He was probably waiting for her already.

She was surprised to see an old man smiling while sitting on a park bench, excited from the early morning fresh air. He was the boy's favourite old friend who usually guarded his bag under and with whom he rarely missed the opportunity to meet in the park. But now the boy loved somebody else who now had the responsibility of the bag without given a prior information to his old friend. The old man was not happy with the development and felt reluctant to speak with her, but she still admired him. The boy came and when he saw and mentioned her, his eyes flamed with joy. She reciprocated. Finally they left for the shop which they had earlier agreed to visit.

Upon reaching the shop, everything appeared not for sale; rather it seemed like a fair with viral marketing technique. Sellers were carrying different sign boards attached to their goods. The buyers went directly to the sellers to negotiate, and if they arrived at a compromise, a contract representing the value of the goods would be made with a chip. The customer received his goods as a consignment sent to his home or office. Therefore, couriering was a very lucrative and special job. The suppliers were called contractors, without whom no commercial transaction could be done.

On their way back home, they saw a huge park which stretched downwards in the direction they were going. It was not an ordinary park but a small, mountainous oasis in the city, which was normally used in organizing special weekly outdoor events, which everyone could attend freely without any restrictions. Numerous meadows stretched to the mountains. Children, adolescents, and adults scattered on the small hills and hollows, entwining with one another.

Guests could draw or write during break times in this show of sorts, and create whatever they were able. Inspiring one another, each artist enriched his or her work while others got encouragement for new ideas about their works. They rediscovered other talents in themselves, which they sometimes brought along with them to exchange with their current work. These shows had national significance and were essential events that built and enriched every individual. Musicians, singers and dancers came all over from this land to participate and to learn also to utilize variety of musical instruments.

The pattern of government and social structure of all countries was the same as in the country where the boy lived. That was the reason why people accepted each other more like people living in different cities rather than different states, since their differences were merely in the physical space, not in the social ambient and, as a result, their mentality was similar. The international gatherings and events, which were constantly being held in each country, also contributed to these similarities.

People from different countries were warmly welcomed. They came to discuss and solve problems of each country together, and to prevent any country from indulging occasionally in a bit of nationalist sabre-rattling.

Dide

The girl had learned a lot that day. It was already dusk and the long day had made them tired, so they decided to go back home. While inside the house, she sat very close to the fire and was filled with the desire to return to that fantastic park again.

Otherland

Chapter 15

Recognition

Tiny petals from the blossoming tree outside swung from the light breeze and fluttered in the air. The thoughts in her head seemed to fly away at the same speed and a number of confessions sprang into her soul. How far away was she from her homeland which she missed in her own way, somewhere deep down!

In this new place, she was finding things similar to but also different from her homeland. She was living in paradox, being in an unknown land that looked very similar to her planet, but was difficult to understand. These contradictions echoed in her, and kept disturbing the peace which she needed to enjoy the beauty before her eyes. A part of her wanted to build a home herself here, without knowing a place suitable to live. She felt like travelling, but felt stuck in one place more than ever. She was looking for a place that could never be exchanged. That was the dilemma enveloping her heart in a veil. Where and how was this supposed to happen? She still felt like a traveler, although she was stuck in one place more than ever. The unbearability of her current sojourn was due to the fact that she had been looking for a place that she wouldn't exchange for any other! This search caused her to be constantly on the move—even in this new land.

Whether the new land or the old one would be this home she'd been looking for was still unknown. She decided to go to the northern part of the house which faced the street. This street ran up a rising hill which stood some distance away from the house.

Otherland

This hill had always been a favourite sporting place for many people with its blue-pink elevator and white lights, which always showed bright yellow tracks of overflying aircrafts. These airplanes flew silently and were shaped like gold and copper capsules. On top of the roof were perched gray turtledoves, which from time to time enjoyed the sounds made by these aircrafts, and thus kept singing. If there was no flight, then the turtledoves remained silent.

Because it was forbidden to drive vehicles on this hill, visitors could only reach it by foot. This allowed as many birds as possible from various species to dwell there. They were attracted by the movements of people walking or jogging. All were accustomed to one another. On rare occasions, the turtledoves clustered as a flock, turning like a tornado.

People did sports there mainly very early in the morning, or late in the afternoon.

This hill was not the only place for sports; there were many parks and stadiums, but people preferred the hill mostly because it afforded the opportunity to perform sporting activities like climbing, jumping and kicking, which could never be done successfully anywhere else. They required a lot of extreme training to master their complexity but also nourished the body.

While she was thinking and staring at this hill, the weather started getting darker. Although the colour of darkness there looked different from the darkness of the Earth, the sense of gloom continued to linger in her as she wandered into an impenetrable night. When the sun went down and the night came, the darkness started to influence people and objects in different ways, depending on if they were good or bad.

The beginning of everything was naturally good. That is why only bad people were considered sick. They would suffer malice and vengefulness. It was a matter of basic upbringing and good manners to take special care of sick people, because every healthy person felt it was their duty to help sick people and to treat them with kindness.

In the darkness of the night, however, the negative side could never be seen, but was lost in the colour of the darkness. So, all sick people as well as bad people became invisible, unlike animals, whose whole nature was good. When an animal died, it became invisible in the darkness; death had deprived all their goodness. Invariably, houses were visible, because the home was always good, despite the type of people living in

Dide

there. The only difference was that in the cases when bad (or in other words sick people) lived in a house, there was no light coming from its windows. If one was suffering form a physical condition like a cold or a broken limb that didn't make them a sick person in the same meaning of the word that people there used to describe evil people, soaking in soul malice.

Trees, grasses, roads were also shining and covered with light.

Bad objects were only the broken ones, lost in the darkness. Thus no street lamps were needed at night, because everything was light, except it was in the distance. This main detail of glowing in the dark made everything good equally visible only when one approached it. Because of that, everyone who was walking at night looked like a walking lantern> If the person was healthy, the shining light around him or her would come from the surrounding objects.

Distance remained always dark, whether there was good or bad, but when closer, good things were always illuminated vividly. If they were bad, then were hidden in the dark spots of the evil, which was a necessary step for healing. The darkness reduced crime, in which such conditions were very difficult to develop. This made the police rarely involved.

Meanwhile, the sky was filled with purple and pale pink before the rising of the sun, but in the background, bright green lines could be easily seen. Against this colourful background of the sky, which lasted for only three hours, one could see bright green streaks. These lines were a result of the sharp movements of stars before disappearing from the sky to pave way for the coming morning. This differed each night because their movements were never repeatable. Each star moved constantly in this land. When the sun started to rise, the sky maintained the same colours like on Earth. During these hours before sunrise, the fairy purple with green furrows became visible. Seeing and watching all of these marvellous and miraculous colours made her sink into them, so as to lose her concentration and forget her homesickness.

The day filled her with the sensation as if she had returned there, or rather as if she hadn't gone far from the Earth, because the morning was the same as in her childhood.

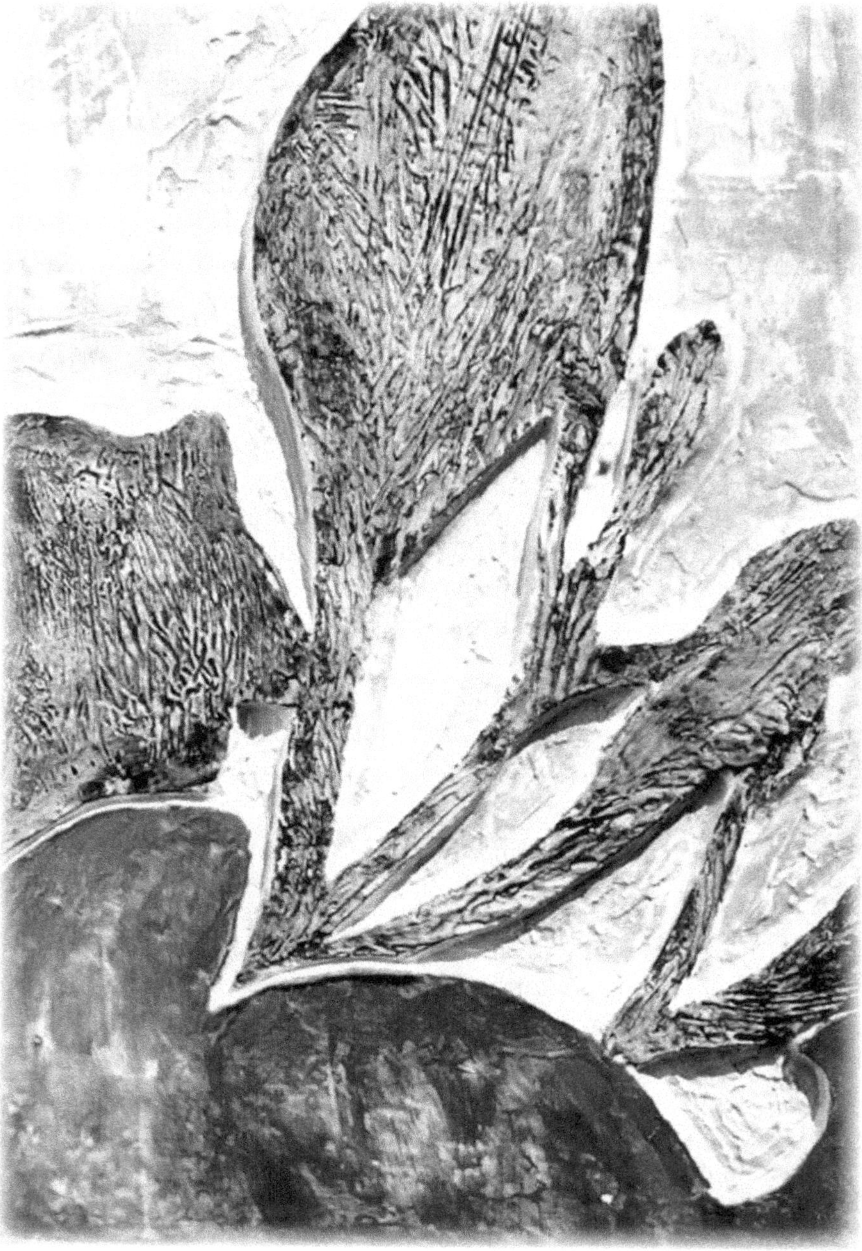

Chapter 16

Memories and Future

Events which occurred in her childhood lingered in her mind.

She seemed to have felt the scent, the aroma and even the taste and that made her feel nostalgic and she turned into the girl she had once been. She managed to recreate in the present the same conditions or situations from her memories in which she had experienced beautiful moments and then she had succeeded in cheating time. She would embrace her childhood, believing everything could be as before when she had been a little girl, embracing her favorite classmate whom she had missed during the summer holiday.

But even though this embrace had the same fragrance as in the past, it was not the same embrace between those two little girls. It simply recreates the embrace of the past in the present moment, when the little girl had grown up and could only, as an adult parent, embrace another little girl who reminded her of her classmate from the past with whom she had shared the same desk.

At the moment of that hug between an adult and a girl, the girl realized that she had grown up and was now capable of hugging as a parent with a tender loving care. And though it was so alive that day, the scent of the leather bag of the kid from the childhood memories and she could feel every detail with all her senses, she was forced to confess that she remained just an adult with her memories at the time of which, so far back in time, where she could never, ever go back.

Yet she knew she could truly touch every memory of hers only if she let it live deep down in her. This was the only place where she could meet her memories and they were as real as they were in the past, when they had happened for the first time in the reality back then.

Only in that reality did the moments from the past repeat themselves, breathing life into them, because her reality of today was real only for the new present and unique moment which was constructing her future.

It was then that she realized that her childhood had been a happy event for the time when she had been a little girl, while at present she was a grown-up and, as such, she could be happy again, cherishing every moment of adulthood she had embraced. Because this was her present in which she could and she wanted to find every piece of happiness, while she had to leave childhood to children, so they could find their happy moments in it. Only when they have grown up themselves would they have the chance to embrace her happiness of an adult, which she was enjoying now.

She acknowledged that those memories were irrevocable and could never go away. But this other land was the only place where she remembered them. Giving them life today was like bringing the past into the present, which would build her real future.

While thinking, she remembered that she would be going out tonight. This brought some confusion because of her tiredness and the urge to sleep: it was already midnight. She thought it was wise to start getting ready, wishing to look beautiful tonight. Just then the boy appeared and became astonished after seeing her awake. He realized that he had failed to explain every important detail about the plan last night.

In this land, people were used to something called "freakish-pure nightlife." Instead of clubbing at midnight, it was done at five o'clock in the morning, when they usually met in an open air restaurant. There they started the day with a delicious breakfast and hot coffee which roused their sensations.

Typically, these bars or restaurants were located at the foot of the hills, which stretched to the top in transparent corridors. These transparent corridors could only to be opened or closed from the roof, depending whether the weather was good or bad. Therefore people ate and drank along the entire length of this long transparent bar.

The glass corridor was divided into sectors, isolated from one another down to transparent doors through which people could use to go into clubs that played different types of music. By climbing upward and passing through the glass which led to area with numerous bars, people could enjoy not only different types of food or drink but also could view nature from outside through the transparent walls of the tubular bar.

Owing to the fact that the hill was steep, from there people could go backward to the foot of the hill by running down a very colourful and cheerful slide, which gently took people into another room with large feathery pillows and huge television screens. If one got tired, there was a resting room or one could be driven back home to spend the whole afternoon in lazy relaxation.

After taking her shower she started remembering the emotions that this beautiful transparent tubular bar had brought her.

Otherland

Chapter 17

The Sun's shadow

The sun had sunk behind the clouds and the grayness so typical of such overcast days cast the shadow of the sun which enveloped everything around. This shadow, or the earthly cloudiness as we often call it, had a particular smell here.

She sensed the invisible heat of the sun that bore a reminiscent fragrance of resin pine. She was excited and surprised to notice how the cloudy weather had taken on an image of the air like running water, and thus kept forming circles around her ankles. This happened in the air like in a puddle. But the shadows were similar in colour, like a smoke of fire in a fog. The mountains rose as if dipped in a milky blanket, formed by the long shadows which the peaks cast over each other.

People, houses and other objects had taken the image of the same smoke, which occasionally looked paler or more saturated. An overhead pedestrian bridge across the river had this similar shadow also. The gelatinous fluid in this river appeared frozen, its reflection was as clear as a mirror.

She walked with him towards the bridge. Her attention was drawn to the argument of two people already on the bridge. She saw how their reflections on the river dimmed. No one was impressed by this strange development, no one dared to pay any attention to them. The boy shrugged his shoulders as if it was something necessary and natural. He went further to explain that on this planet, bridges were the only place where people met to argue. For the past several years the buzz among those who had taken more than a passing interest in this trend had been enormous. Each of the two opposing parties had its own bench, which the other was forbidden to step on while disputing. Their quarrel could be dragged as far as was necessary, but could only be done in the middle of the bridge. If either party was tired, even if they had not finished completely laying out their grievances, then one could only withdraw.

The shadows of the arguers were always smudged on the river surface. A clear reflection of the people on the surface of the river was the criterion for a real truce. If they had resolved their disputes and entered into a real agreement then surely their reflections would become clear and well-defined. No one ever paid attention or intervened. Everyone had been there or would be there someday in the future. This bridge had been solely built for this purpose.

Meanwhile trees alongside of this bridge were noted for their pale green and white stems covered with yellow mushrooms. These globular entities were honeycombs for bees in this land.

And the bees were tinted in purple and a ball-like shape as were the honeycombs which they built and filled with honey that people really loved to eat. Looking at the crown of those white trees with no leaves, she remained there staring at the stark contrast, which was reveled among their light branches and the deep, crystal clear, intense blue sky, all wrapped in the mildness of a warm sunny day, which seemed to have chased away all the clouds and grayness.

She was marvelling.

Dide

Otherland

Chapter 18

Waking Up

Every day we wake up and fall asleep again, sometimes it's a bit difficult, sometimes it's easy, fast or slowly, but one circle repeats with the different tints of its cycle.

Here on this planet people experienced two mornings each day: early morning and the hours before noon. Then the second new day began without ever having had a night. Time ran faster but was not doubled, because one of the days was equal to two-and-a-half of those days. Instead, one evening was missed every two days. Then the cycle started again during the beginning of the first day and after the noon of the following morning that ended the night of the second day.

This made life easy and delightful. People used the night to allow the great energy powerhouse enough time to recover, and to avoid thoughts and motivations outside of human awareness.

She noticed that two-and-a-half days had passed but it looked like a day. She was having a saturated feeling of satisfaction about things around her and never noticed the day was running faster. This was nice and beneficial. After such a long period of sleeping and waking up, she decided to ask him a question that had been bothering her:

What brought him to her Earth and how did he happen to find her?

While they were sitting and chatting, she was thinking that two weeks had already passed since she had come to live here on his planet.

Her question made him think, as if puzzled at what had happened to him, since he didn't have a reasonable explanation for it.

He wasn't sure, but began to tell a story. This event was destined to happen in his life until it was sufficient to form and become a story, and could only be taken away by itself.

This beginning was not initiated by a moment or a day, but had been kind of created all his life, until it was fully shaped to hit the road of its own accord.

In the beginning he was trained as a pilot. But one cannot become a pilot in a day. That's why he believed that he had been preparing for years for what he at that moment telling her to happen.

Right from his childhood he had always dreamed of flying so as to see all objects from the sky, like houses and mountains. And this feeling had taken over control of his life, while looking up to the sky. His first flight might not be so long or brilliant, but he was created to do this, and other dreams and desires could never stop him from this flying ambition.

He studied aviation as a happy student. And he wished that what he had studied and trained for would turn into a reality. His teachers and coaches had always believed in his talent and capability. And he had always believed in himself and had never spared any effort to get his tasks done.

Sometimes the boy had been completely drained of his strengths and was brought to utter exhaustion and at the edge of desperation because of the helplessness which he had to face alone, tackling, at the end of his tether, yet another task assigned to him. That boy had always believed in himself and had never spared himself to achieve success. But the endless and repetitive exams started to seem the same, as if requiring from him to prove the same achievements over and over again. They didn't lead him forward. On the contrary, they were holding him back, turning into an impediment which prevented him from getting where he would have been long before, if they hadn't stopped him. He had felt strong, realizing he was squandering his strength for such insignificant things like the repetitive, exhausting exams. He felt that his strength was much bigger and deserved to conquer something huge and new. So, after yet another moment of exhaustion, he made a decision that he would embark on a trip on his own since he had sensed for a very long time that he was ready for it.

Dide

If he had stopped sometime earlier, before embarking on his aviation course, the situation would have been different.

Besides, soon he would be going on a journey to an unknown planet as it was destined and made known to him by his ancestors. One of those stories was about the Earth planet, which was presumed to be father of his planet.

Many centuries ago, after a cosmic disaster, half of Earth was torn and lost in the universe. And now, the two planets were lost to one another. Half was his land, where she was right now. He rightly would not say if the planet in which she came from was the Earth of legend. But he did say that if he ever flew an airplane one day, no one would ever know of his departure, because everything was going to be secret.

Thus one early morning, he got on his airplane and flew into an unknown direction. No one knew of his departure. He had decided to fly further than anyone had done before. In this land, nobody was allowed to fly alone beyond an unknown distance, but he did in order to defeat negative feelings that had kept him down for years. While he was on his route, he concentrated with his whole mind and this made him to go further until he got into another planet.

On his own planet, everything moved continuously towards an invisible corridor. And the stars were constantly orbiting without repeating their directions.

That was the reason that the science of the stars there was more like a science of their movement and not of the stars themselves, because they were countless and every night appeared new and unknown. And the sun on this planet revolved around it, following its movements. So the boy, while flying on his own in the outer space, leaving his planet in the unfathomable distance behind, understood that all that uncharted space he was crossing is a place constantly changing and everything it would reveal to him was new and unknown to him. This cosmos was radiance full of glitter and color coming from the tails of passing matter, shapeless, but possessing strength which allowed them to move, filling the space and leaving a stunningly beautiful color trail behind.

Flying through these colours was fantastic a dream accomplished. He was so eager to see where this might bring him. The planets were easily recognizable from afar because they were wrapped in darkness which was their own cosmos.

Soon he was able to recognize the reputed darkness that surrounded Earth, where she originated. He saw the green speck and decided to dash into the orbit.

He was fascinated by his discovery, and realizing its potential, he quickly set his sights to capture the glimpse of the newfound land. At the beginning, this planet reminded him of his own planet. And then, while walking on the newfound land, he wondered where he was and suddenly he saw the girl whose shoelace was untied. At that moment he was sure it was a foreign land.

After their brief conversation, their kiss had somehow carried them back to his planet.

Both were now listening to each other's stories and were puzzled by the instinct or magic behind the kiss. He now saw the universe and his life as a miracle which was able to happen on his own planet as part of his dream of this girl of the other land.

Chapter 19

Smart Folly

It was his wish to trust her; therefore, he sought a way to prove that he had much confidence in her. He knew he had to leave her alone to make her own decision. But he wanted his choice to be known to her too.

Trust didn't tolerate requirements or any forms of violence towards the other in order to teach the other what their right choice was. This was something everyone had to decide on their own with their own free will. Without this freedom it wouldn't have been his choice, but hers. He was longing for her to give him her choice. He was craving to see her happy, wanting him, getting attached to him with all her heart, which he found enough to love him and give him happiness, the same happiness that had already been born in his soul. He was probably in love, but he wanted to feel loved and needed.

He encouraged her to be driven alone around the city in his car, which looked like a yellow ball with one white and two blue ribbons running the entire length. He wanted her to have her private life and the freedom to make the choice that led back to him. And this freedom, he believed would serve as a core framework upon which all passions could be derived so as to enjoy her stay.

As she was driving one day, she happened to glance through the side mirror. The whole city appeared quiet and peaceful. She could only see the wet, illuminated street, with neither traffic nor pedestrians passing by. She was calm and settled and thought only of good things;

love preoccupied her whole mind. She felt purified by the dampness and pulled the car over by the side of the street next to the boy's home. She decided to walk.

A woman on a bicycle with two pedals on a platform, without tires, rode by. The platform slid along the surface of the ground, thereby making the ride slower but lubricating. As she pondered this extraordinary development, her attention was drawn towards an elderly man who was walking his dog, which looked as old as his master, as beautiful and perhaps as noble.

As the dog ran up to her, she started playing with it. This motivated the master to stop and canter on about the weather. It was summer time, when people usually travelled. But this summer, everyone had chosen to stay behind and enjoy the holidays like he had done for years. He said it seemed strange that this new trend had overtaken his fellow citizens and became the centre of their planning.

Their conversation was typical as if they were strangers from the neighbourhood who had met by chance and who were discussing, in a friendly manner, interpersonal relationships and matters that excited them and, in this way, they were kind of updating their watches to have the exact time and then, saying goodnight, they would part. The same was the conversation of the girl with the unknown neighbour that she had met.

He talked of religion, raising questions about people and their faiths. "Tomorrow is Saturday," stated the man after talking about the liturgy in church, which normally took place every Saturday. There were many churches on this planet, because people loved to go and worship their God.

People gathered in these buildings not to show off or be seen by their neighbours and acquaintances, but because of their faith in their Creator. They believed that he had created all of them and everything that was surrounding them. They wanted to share their love with Him and with the congregations. They had encouraged one other to overcome their difficulties and share their successes and joys with one another. This had always fostered unity, peace and solidarity among them. But more than anything else, the peace which they had in themselves came out of the belief that they must love God, who had helped them in many ways. This love they believed was indispensable and filled their days with gratitude.

Soon the dog started barking at one of the neighbours' kitten, which appeared behind the window of a house nearby. This dispute between the barking dog and hissing cat thwarted further questions. It was only reasonable for the youngster to continue his walk with his dog in order not to disturb his neighbours with this harmless dog fuss. So the girl parted from the man and remained alone. She stared at the kitten which now seemed calm and even happy after the departure of the dog which wouldn't do it any harm anyway except for irritating itself with its barking. She was enjoying her dinner, as if having completely forgotten to think of anything whatsoever. Imperceptibly time had passed and she lost track of it, not knowing how long she had been sitting there, staring pensively at the window, where the kitten had disappeared a long time before. All of a sudden, she got back to her senses and thoughts rushed into her head.

She missed the boy. She couldn't even understand why he had to send her on her own on this evening walk around the town. She was in doubt whether he needed to stay alone. She began to rediscover the night falling over the town, although it looked like any other night before that one. She had enough of walking and decided to go back to the boy's, who had grown impatient for a couple of hours at home, where he was waiting eagerly for her return.

She wanted a truly perfect world with a profoundly perfect reality, which would stir immaculately perfect feelings in her, shared with people who demonstrated flawless relationships with each other. The unknown planet seemed to offer all that. Then again, something was missing. Then she suddenly realized that he loved her and this acquired a greater meaning than the perfection she was longing for.

Otherland

JE T'AIME !

Chapter 20

Easily Done

She finished working on an embossment which was done with constant attention and great devotion. The design was ambitious, but to her, it was not only an embossment, more like a simple object to which she gave a soul and freedom. But she didn't understand the power behind its production. Somehow she had revealed the hidden beauty deep inside it, making them eye-catching wonder of artistic creativity.

Obviously, by creating the simplest ordering which was needed by someone, she gave herself an extraordinary wealth, which changed her all over and uncovered worlds full of surprises hidden somewhere deep inside her. The things she would consider small had the capacity to surprise her in an unusual and unique way, creating huge amazement in her soul which helped her create more such small things, bringing the great wonders she needed to feel truly happy like she had once dared dream of.

She cherished her work and wished it to grow into an engine of growth to move further up the grid. She knew she was naive in her dreams sometimes, but selfless in her desires, which made her pursue her goals more fervently.

She was talented and it was a huge blessing, but she had to look after it and work hard to keep it healthy and growing through the years, just like a happy child needs to grow up and turn into a real star. This blessing was her true friend, giving her safety and turning her into a more self-sacrificing person, helping and encouraging her and immensely loved by the rest. Some people live calmly and wisely, which makes their lives full of dignity. Others are filled with calmness because of the impersonality which makes their days drag by. There is another group of people who live their lives as if in a merry race, laughing with life, carrying their freedom and burning with loving hearts. She was such a cheerful girl, naïve in her dreams at times, but always unselfish in her desires, which made her pursue her aims purposefully, but also always taking a step back and showing charity. Charity is like a powerful ointment that will heal all wounds. It is force that will make the strongest elements in the human soul kneel before it.

While some embossed plates had a dark beige band, others had thinner bands in lighter colours of ochre. This appeared to her like the borders in the human body. Looking at the color spots formed by the streaks, one could probably find the boundary of our souls, which made them narrow, turning us into petty, fussy people, drawing thick, clearly defined lines—the borders of our forgiveness and love which are supposed to be boundless because this is how we are created to be in our immaculate inception. Besides, she had combined the transformatory power of art with the talent she embellished so as to bring happiness to the people. The plates were also made as surprise she was eager to give out, as they were apt for the city's forthcoming holiday. Each home installed a specially designated mailbox for this occasion in which people could place gifts for people living in that house.

The different coloured images on these small plates signified unity and togetherness to the people living in whichever home received them.

The tiny color tiles, with different images on them, carried the feeling of unity and togetherness of the people living in the house that received them, because everyone knew that the other is a key part of the reason for this gift being given in the first place. No one calculated their contribution, because everyone was too busy and preoccupied in their task to feel happy and enjoy the presence of the other family members. In this way people didn't find it difficult to be happier and more caring towards their neighbours in the street, because they were always like that in their own homes.

Dide

The colourful gifts were later hung or glued to the wall in bedrooms, thus making a wall of colourful plates. And these reminded them every morning for the love for one another.

Children also had the right to receive some of these gifts and later put them on the wall in their bedrooms. Each year, every child was entitled to one coloured plate. This way, while the children were growing up, one could know their age by the colour tiles in their nursery room. This holiday was celebrated once a year, though at different times for each town, but absolutely every year each kid received one tiny colour tile. When they became adults and built a home, then all those plates received as a gift were taken to the new home as a symbol of tradition which showed that the child was loved by everyone, from generation to generation.

After putting her hand in her bag, the girl noticed the last and best plate now went to the mailbox of the boy's home. She wished to express her love to the boy in particular and the whole household in general with this colourful gift, even if she was a guest from a different planet.

Otherland

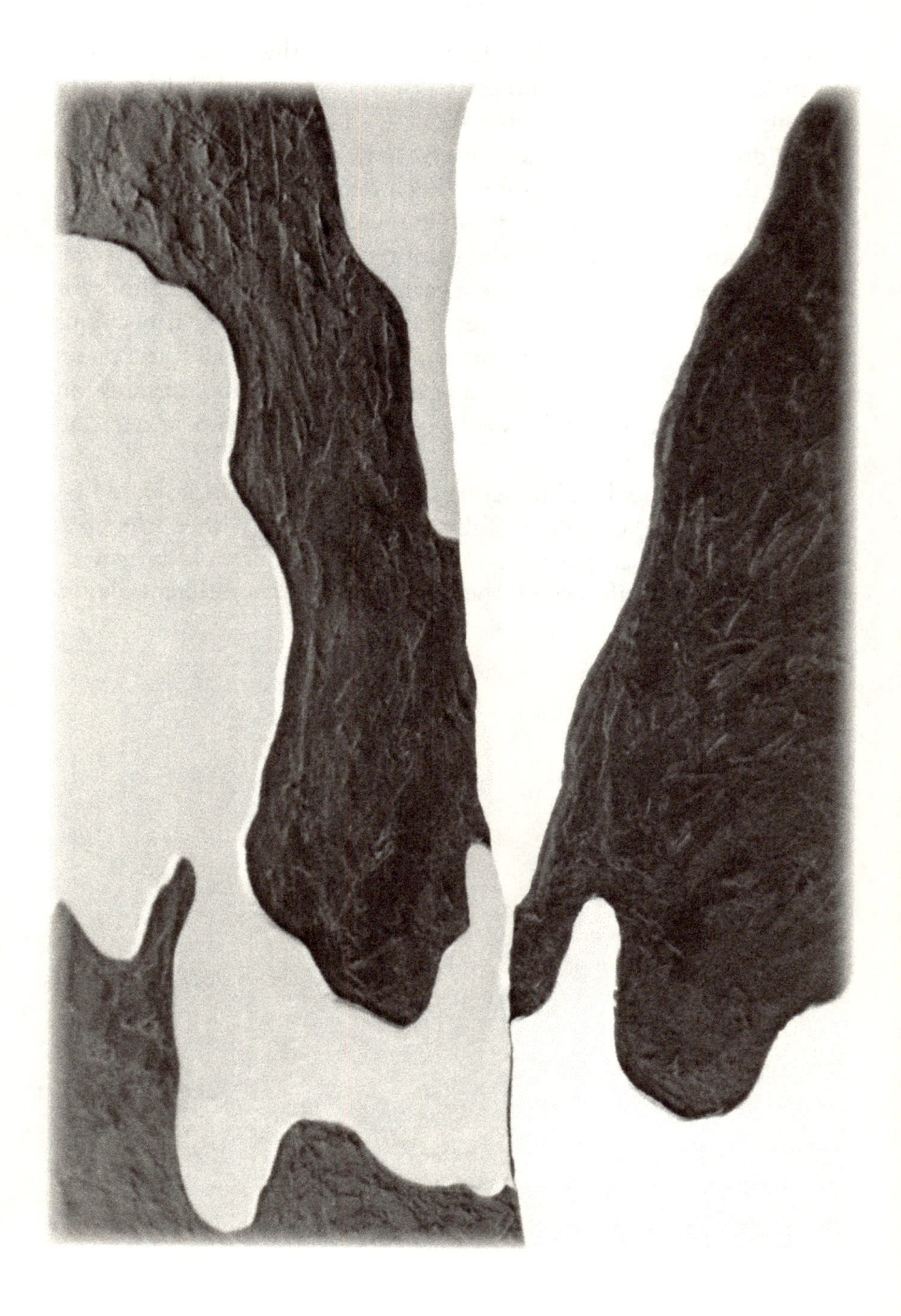

Chapter 21

Without Words

The desire to express her love was so tremendous, because of the happiness he had given to her. She wanted to say words born out of tenderness and care for someone, who she would sacrifice all she had for, so that this person could receive happiness as a present. Deep down in her soul she longed for being good. This happiness ushered in a new era of tranquillity, therein liberating her from bitterness and painful stigma that formerly provoked fears in her life.

She was born again in herself, turning into a different, more beautiful girl. In a quite ordinary silence, her dreams imprinted inside of her, turning her into an image of them. And all this happened without anyone's words being spoken. Even she could not find words in herself which, to give birth to the need to be spoken. She was reveling in her quietness and even more in the striking change which happened without words, but so beautifully before her very own eyes, in her soul and everywhere around her! The doldrums that had filled her minutes started feeling not as emptiness in time, but as a golden opportunity to embrace the changes she didn't have time for before, but she never stopped longing for.

Though no one was watching her, she began to go deep into her soul, scattering and rearranging the words, concepts and ideas that had taken hold of her. She laboured so hard, as if thousands eyes were on her, waiting to see what she was able to create.

Even she didn't know what this work of hers would turn into, but she was convinced that she had to put in effort and walk the road to a new change which would give her new strength, new knowledge and beliefs that would make her an intrinsic part of a new world. This new world would become her reality which would bestow on her the truly beautiful home she had been dreaming of.

She wanted a new start in her life in this new special place where she could feel secure, safe and could be in her own home, built with love. She started working quietly in her loneliness, which had turned out to be her best friend. She identified her gaps and knowledge that was necessary for this purpose.

She would find the gaps in the knowledge she needed. She racked her brain over difficult problems and she would do them over and over again until she solved them. Around that time, she stopped looking for the others, because she dedicated herself to the not so easy task of rediscovering herself, so that she could have new eyes through which to see the others; eyes that would be able to spot personalities she had missed up to that point.

It seemed as though those changes happened really slowly in her and the problems she was trying hard to solve were obviously more difficult than she had expected. Their solutions drove her farther away from her dreams about the success of a happy change. There wasn't much emotion in this purposeful work she was doing. Her conviction to stick to the road ahead and the direction its pointed, helped her maintain prudence and to discover her abilities step by step, managing to master them with the small, recent achievements, the fruits of which hadn't ripened yet.

She put all her effort into not giving up her silent endeavour. There was something ancient, passed on by her ancestors, which she wanted to recreate so that it could be rediscovered in the new world. She wanted it to be represented in a way that would allow its understanding in the same way as the meaning of the message her painting carried. She remembered her childhood and the things that amazed her in it.

She remembered during her childhood days, the things that amazed her were things inside the house of her grandfather, and they looked different when her grandparents were still alive. As a little child, those painted walls seemed to her like a fairytale castle. She had never seen such a beautiful wall anywhere else. The inspiration she got from them made her kept staring at them each time and she admired the skills of her grandfather, who had done the paintings. Then she started dreaming of creating even more magnificent and beautiful paintings with new skills when she became an adult.

Awakened by this memory, she now engage herself with the idea of transforming one of the walls in the hallway of the boy's home to show the culture of her own world. She hoped that this would make him smile on the beauty of her childhood, recreated with love from her planet and represented by her own style and talent, by revealing insight about her genetic makeup as well as the wisdom and blessings which she had inherited. Talents and characters were meant to belong to their respective owners. She used words from the language that was spoken and understood by the people of his planet, but embellished them in such a unique way to create an eye-popping impression.

She did begin to paint the words of a story on one of the walls. Her story was a fanciful account and embellished with illustrations. It appeared more like a parable or fairytale which was normally read to children going to bed. But she used a new writing technique that never existed in her world. Her story was at least as old as the memories she had when she was a child.

This story was painted like that: There was once a girl that lived in the house of her grandparents.

Her grandmother had taught her how to knit hats for dolls and her grandfather helped her to discover the world of letters and numbers.

The girl liked dipping a finger in the pot of honey which her grandfather used to fill from the beehives he owned. More than anything else she enjoyed the moments she used to spend with her granddad, because he always encouraged her in everything she was trying to learn, helping her to find the answers to her child-like questions. He would also praise every childhood achievement of hers, which encouraged her to succeed even more, as if in that way she demonstrated her endless love for him, constantly growing in her little child-like soul. Every smile of his and every hug was irrefutable proof to her that he loved her in return and not less than she loved him. This was how she used to spend her summer and a magical summer it was, because of the games she would play with her granddad, searching in every new day to discover and learn something new, so that she could gift-wrap her small achievements and present them to her granddad, eager for his approval and looking up to him in awe and admiration.

He would never fail to reward her with his warmest and hugest hug. That would make her dream about becoming so famous one day when she grew up, that her granddad would be really proud of her, presenting her with the greatest reward of all: his loving smile and warm look which would reveal how proud he was of her achievement.

But the summer hadn't even come to an end when her grandfather suddenly died. She didn't understand death back then. That's why, to her, his absence seemed like a distant journey which made her sad, but her granddad was always alive in her mind and heart. Her granddad was no longer by her side, but her dreams remained. She vowed to achieve as big a success as was her love for her beloved granddad and that love was huge, almost boundless.

She grew up with the same love which would forever leave a trace of confidence in her so that she could manage to overcome anything and make her big dream come true. One day she did grow up and did give her granddad the greatest gift of all: Her achievements, though he was no longer by her side and she couldn't see his smile, which had always been the solid proof of her being loved and which had always been enough to make her happy.

Remembering him, she successfully painted and transformed all these coloured letters and numbers onto the wall. Invariably, people here hung pictures on the walls but not letters. The boy was delighted as well as amazed with her beautiful gift of the Earthly story. The technique which she used in her painting was somehow familiar to him and also to the entire household in general. She used an innovative material that had never been used before on Earth, which was newly discovered here in the new world. Everyone loved to read the story, which on its own provided tremendous insight into the human diversity across the two planets.

They would smile and that would bring warmth into their souls and they would fall asleep with more faith in their dreams and more love for each other.

Chapter 22

The Narrator

Whoever narrates a story always wishes to bring it to a conclusion. He loves to tell what happens, without telling more than could be inferred from the story's action. He wishes to describe the relation in which he stands to the story, to spot the importance of seemingly insignificant details, and to weave disparate strands of information into meaningfulness.

There is a topic he wants to discuss, but he cannot find an interpreter. Besides he wants to discuss it first with himself. He wants to be the first to listen to the story. In fact, the storyteller is a zealous listener, but only for the story that only he himself can create. This ability of his to listen and tell a story simultaneously makes him capable of creating and writing stories which are poetic descriptions of feelings and scenery or quickly changing events.

Telling a story on alien planet was like magic because the story itself seemed like steam which rose from a hot cup. The words would not only sound, but that vapour from the steam would be inhaled to keep one warm so as to be able to understand or perceive not only the surface but also the deeper level of meaning of the whole story.

Before the boy brought her to the theatre, he did not explain it very well, but she loved the beautiful stories that were presented. He had wished to show her the magic of this art which fascinated him so much, like her painted letters on the wall. The theatre was built in a large open-air space, staged in one of the most spectacular stadiums she

Otherland

had ever seen. The language spoken by the people here sounded like her language, but the difference in words and its meanings were often misunderstood by her. Therefore she sought help often from him and he explained the meanings of the words to her.

They sat comfortably in one of the last rows, where the whole scene was viewable from above and wonderful. The hills nearby were also visible from there, and these brought a freshness to the audience. The stadium was filled with thousands of people who sat silently waiting for the theatre to open.

The actors appeared and bowed to the silent stadium which was animated by the applause. Then they went behind red veil and the audience froze again in anticipation. The white stage was lit with white and blue lights.

A beautiful girl dressed like a white flower with yellow cuffs on her thin hands, fluttering like petals.

She appeared as to have sprouted into the stage. Then she began to dance. The sounds of the music were similar to majestic eagles seen above the firmament of the Earth. The ballerina's movement was evolving the light and grace of the music. Then the other actors joined. By making the music a background of the speech heard in the play, the distinctive musical voice drifted pass pleasantly to the audience.

The actors' clothing was, black, orange, white or yellow to dark brown. They were telling a story about a butterfly, from her inception as a caterpillar to pupa and then into a beautiful creature with stretched wings, swung by the wind and later attracted by the nectars of colourful flowers.

This was a beautiful earthly story, known to everyone, but told so compellingly and performed extremely colorfully and enchantingly. The girl forgot to notice the words she failed to understand, because the actors' performance led her through the story which was coming to life and dancing before her very eyes.

The audience was enthralled by the rhythm of the music. The show ended with smiling, bowing from the actors and wild applause from the audience. The viewers left with excitement and also with sadness that it was over.

After this emotional show, the boy took her gently by her hand and wished to show her the greenhouse belonging to his parents, where flowers were grown and later brought to market. His parents were extremely earthly people who worked hard in their land, turning it into a paradise; hence they were not dreaming of starry adventures or exploring others planets, like their son. They had always supported him in his ambitions, but were never diverted from their obligations to their colourful gardens and greens.

Inside and outdoor the gardens were full of flowers, shrubs and small trees, used to fill the flower shops in and around the districts in this planet. On many occasion, agencies and other flower shop owners ordered flowers from them.

While walking in between the flower beds on this very sunny day, she was overwhelmed by an irresistible urge to go back home. This prompted her to ask him when they would return back to her planet, explaining about the homesickness.

He stared at her with astonishment but with deep understanding, knowing full well how uneasy she must have felt while staying in his land. He then promised her to embark for the journey in a few days to go back to Earth. She smiled went with him to enjoy the beauty of the flowers.

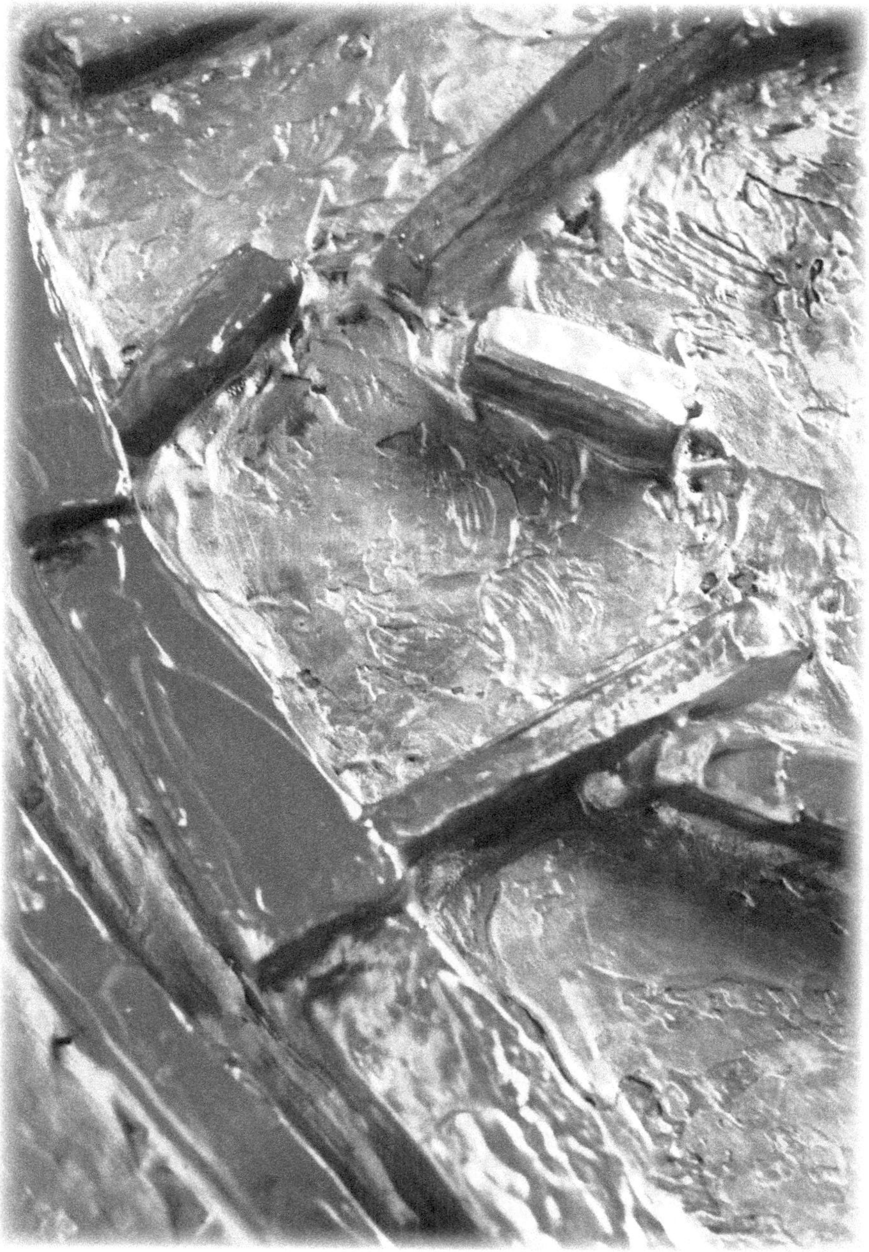

Chapter 23

Something Unknown

His parents gave her several palm seeds as a gift for her journey back to Earth. They explained she could keep only one seed out of the all because under the law of their planet, one was enough to give her every necessary thing she might need. It would be worthwhile to give the remaining seeds away to other people on her planet, for their personal needs and wishes.

Each seed bore a different fruit based on who it was given to and how it has been cared for. She doubted if other people would understand the value and opportunities hidden in the seeds, for these small embryonic plants were known to exhibit a tremendous array of variation.

She couldn't understand how her caring for a seed she sowed would make her most cherished dreams come true.

Though his parents had already been accustomed to his absence, they hoped to see him back soon once he accompanied her back to Earth.

As both were preparing for this forthcoming trip, the news of their departure brought joy to the entire household, thus putting them into another festive mode that motivated loud music and play. Everyone was absolutely happy, singing and dancing while at the same time arranging their suitcases.

They had planned to fly in his airplane. He had already imagined how he would be showing her the beauties of the sky as well as how to navigate to her planet. Now they were only a couple of days away from their departure and he decided to go sailing with her on the river.

It was his favourite adventure since he was a little boy. Now as an adult he still loved to go there frequently. As he was rummaging in his belongings, he accidentally opened a long-forgotten box with photos from his childhood. He believed she might be interesting for her to see some of his childhood toys.

He quickly ran to the hallway, pulled a chest out from the cupboard and opened it as if he wanted to reveal his childhood kingdom to himself. Inside this box were objects that looked bizarre, strange toys with which a little child used to play. Even though they looked so incredible, he still admired and looked at them with great interest. He decided to remove the objects one after the other, to show them to her. He remembered a story about his childhood.

Then there had been a tangle of dried grass twisted in a circle. As a child they were playing traders, using the leaves from trees instead of money. With this money from the branches, he bought a braided grass bracelet from one little girl who played as a salesgirl in a jewellery shop, where jewellery was made from grass and shells of nuts, instead of gold and precious stones.

There was also a bent metal hoop that was rolled on the streets, held by a rod curved at its lower end. There were lots of colourful glass pellets. The boys used them to play one of their favourite games. Several pellets were arranged on the ground to a certain distance and each tried to hit them with his own colourful pellet.

She rummaged through the tiny figurines of different animals with which she started to know and love the animal kingdom.

A wooden furrowed stick protruded out from a pile of animals in the chest. He remembered how he had peeled and carved with his little knife the bark of the wood, forming beautiful patterns on it. He had built a tiny airplane which crashed during an unsuccessful flight from the kitchen table when it fell on the concrete floor, before hit in the cupboard's metal handle. It was a very sad moment for him and he had tried for years to forget about this incident. For years all the broken pieces were hidden and forgotten, and now he sat helplessly on the wooden box, filled with frustration accrued from those broken dreams.

However, she was sitting next to him while listening to all these stories and after seeing the sadness in his eyes she quietly closed the box to disengage his fantasy and bring him back to reality.

He still wished to show her the boat they would be using for sailing tomorrow. They went down to the garage where he had his workshop, boat, engines and other tools all well-arranged on the shelves. They spent some hours there, while he related stories of his previous voyages on the river.

They went back to the house, closed the suitcases they had been packing all day, had dinner and fell asleep, eagerly awaiting the walk that the following day was to bring.

Otherland

Chapter 24

Refreshing Memory

As memories came back, she was becoming more and more certain that this land was a lost part of the Earth.

Since she had arrived on this planet and discovered bizarre answers to questions she'd never before asked, she quite never known what to do with the situation in this land. But how could she return to her own land, having nothing much to tell, instead with just the gift of the wonderful seeds? Her urge to travel had pushed her to cross interstellar space but her love for her native land had begun to gather some momentum. But she and the boy loved each other and whenever they were together she could see how much he needed her and wanted to share his world by revealing all its secrets.

More than anything else she was thinking about the boy. The boy had turned into a big answer which, at the same time, brought questions about past desires that seemed not to excite her any more and a new element erupted in her soul and brought her closer to the boy, seeking his world and loving his desires.

She could get to know only the one she truly loved and she was starting to love him. She didn't know what she was going to do without him in her land and that was one of her new questions. When she had been on her planet, she had longed so much for achieving success so that the others would be really proud of her.

She had wanted to travel far and wide and to experience something extraordinary. She remembered how those thoughts followed and tortured her back then and now she was experiencing all that. And it was quite an achievement to be on an unknown planet and to return to your own after that, bringing all those stories to tell, bringing even presents from the unknown planet, though the presents are just tiny seeds.

It was to happen very soon—she was about to return to Earth and that was to be one of her greatest achievements. Her dream to travel far and away had also come true since she had crossed the interstellar space. And it was quite extraordinary that she had lived happily all those days in a foreign land, but the love for her homeland was about to take her back home. Although she also found a new love in her heart, while discovering and getting to know the smile in the boy's eyes.

She noticed how proud he was with her when introducing her to his friends. He was trying to understand her with her novelties, watching her as if she was some kind of wonderful miracle which he had found himself and it was now changing his life. He remembered the moments when he cherished her as his dream that had come true. He would leave her alone even at moments when he was dying to enjoy her presence. He would do that so that she could feel at ease and not pressured by him, since he wanted more than anything to be accepted by her as her best friend, not as a threat.

He hoped to accompany her back home, though he did not want her returning back. Even with his airplane, he had never flown so high like he had flown in ordinary moments and time spent together with her. He looked with pain to the forthcoming trip, though it would bring about their separation. There would be no room for consideration when tough choices must be made, and there was no option that didn't start with difficult.

In those days while nursing the idea of her return to Earth, she secretly was knitting a scarf for him, weaving in it all the love and contradictions that were germinating within her. She knitted this silver scarf in the quiet moments of night, after he called on her. With this she brought their two planets together and made them into one.

She wanted to make him happy, showing him that while he had been feeling sad thinking that she had been only craving to leave, in fact she had been learning to love him, thinking about him and turning him into a part of herself. In her silvery scarf she had knitted during the moments of their calm conversations in the evenings, when he would tell her through a different perspective the endings of the plans she had been sharing with him. It was with him that she discovered a new world, his world, where she rediscovered herself. The things she liked doing, such as the beautiful drawing of letters on the wall, which she managed to recreate in a different manner here. And though those things brought her joy, her joy was twice as big when she would see the happiness reflected in his eyes. Now he was more important to her than anything else.

Finally, wrapping the scarf around his neck, she whispered her thanks for his hospitality.

His eyes betrayed how much she meant to him. He embraced her but was filled with sad thoughts about her departure which disengaged him from his activities.

Soon his sad thoughts left him and he ran outside to brag to his friends with his new scarf which was now the symbol of a big dream of his that had come true. She found herself alone in the room again, arranging the table for breakfast. The day had started a long time before and they hadn't had breakfast yet. They had to hurry up because today was the day of their walk by the river.

She was smiling.

Otherland

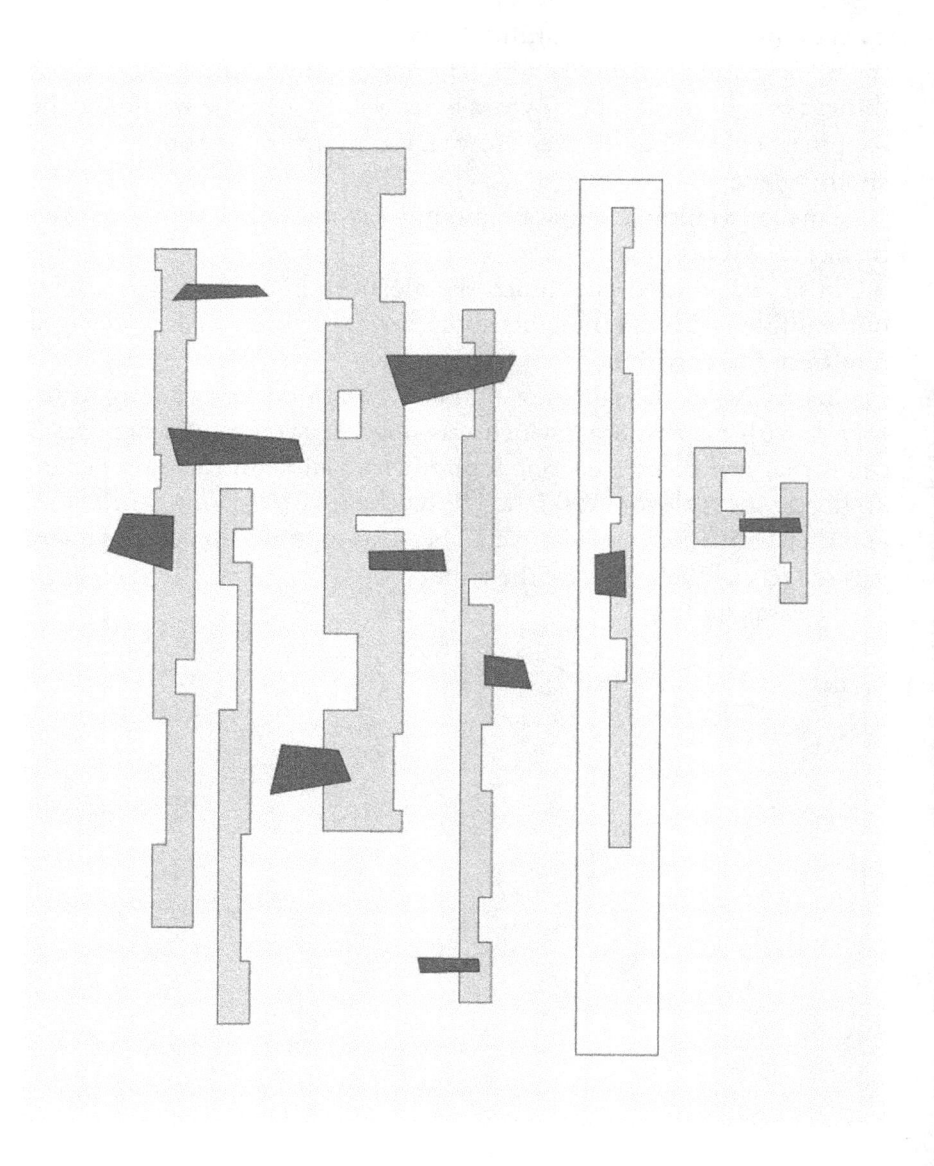

Chapter 25

Ready to Sail

On the following day they set out with the boat and sailed along the tranquil river. He told more stories about his planet and although she had seen some things, it appeared as if she was hearing about them for the first time. Perhaps the gap was caused by the discrepancy in her perception of the world and things around it. Though these differences and misunderstandings about the same events were happening before her eyes, she felt lonely, sad, and misunderstood by him and others too.

He saw her sorrow and told her that until now, she had been watching things happening in and around his life, and as an observer she would not realize the difficulties or joys of what he was going through until she lived in his life. He gave her one of his oars to paddle the boat, and she felt the power of the water.

He told her that if she became his, they would be sharing the same air, food and a common home. Her presence would enable him to love her, and he would turn her heart into a home, where he would dwell and find his happiness.

While she was trying to understand his words, she got lost in her misunderstanding and found herself in the midst of confusion.

At this juncture he kissed her again for the second time. After opening her eyes in the process of taking her lips back from his, she found herself in the same place where they initially met for the first time. She was surprise remember how long ago it had happened.

Her astonishment turned into shock when she realized everything around her was the same as it was upon their first meeting.

The same people stood and moved their eyes like before and were aware of the couple kissing, as if they had not gone away for days or months, but for a few moments in which their kiss lasted.

They met the same day and for the first time in all the time of the girl's journey to the boy's planet there was a wonder hidden in the spell of their kiss. It was a wonderful journey in a world full of unforgettable beauty and events.

They looked up at each other, held hands and understood the secret behind their journey, fully aware that it remained hidden from all the people surrounding them.

There was an unspoken question in his eyes. His desire to travel was taking him away from her and the memories they shared. He wanted to ask her to follow him back to his land.

Without her uttering a word, he was able to read in her eyes that she was to stay here and if he intended to leave he would have to do it without her. His desire to travel pushed him far away from her and their common memories and the craving in his heart for her arms made him plead her to join him on this journey. They couldn't call it a separation because only today they were meeting. It just happened—they had to slowly drop their arms and move on in different directions. He looked sad and disappointed because of her indecisiveness and mad at himself because of his craving for their date, which tortured him and begged him to stay.

He turned his eyes away and pretended to be in a hurry, so as not to miss some other appointments. No one could even suspect that they met and separated at the same split second on that only day of theirs.

She was left alone, while he was on his way back home.

She was enthralled by the memories of a long journey in a foreign land and a heavy sorrow burdened her because she was missing the boy who revealed this world, leaving his dreams and desires forever inside her, giving her the gift of their kiss.

The single day they had spent together had passed like a dream.

The following days she was supposed to convince herself that she was on her own planet. Because her perceptions of the foreign land had been awoken, presenting her with the gift of their feeling and sensations which let her see the surrounding world as never before. She was surprised at the wind and the way it moved all branches without missing a tree around her and at the same time it messed up her hair, which prevented her from seeing, forming a disheveled veil before her eyes.

Once she was so pensively carried away in her memories of the time when she had felt the wind on the unknown planet that she stopped feeling how, on this very day and on her own planet, the wind was also caressing her face. All her sensitivity and feelings had changed. She was enjoying everything that surrounded her to the full now, but deep down she was also sad and nostalgic for all those things she had touched and known on the other planet. She felt sad and pining for a foreign land, situated in the unfathomable distance far away and she was now rediscovering her homeland. This new land was now alive in her mind and heart, being a part of her.

Otherland

Chapter 26

Old Dreams

She had known the other land. She had travelled there accidentally by a kiss. She quietly and consistently organized her thoughts which she brought from a foreign land. And gradually everything started to manifest in her head.

The girl was in her homeland and yet another morning reminded her of all the answers which she had discovered on the boy's planet, as well as the questions that had been born in her soul there. She also remembered her old dreams that had given birth to her previous cravings and questions and started calmly and meticulously to arrange the thoughts she had brought from the foreign land.

Gradually everything started falling into its place and that brought her peace of mind. She mused over the dreamed world, which had once made her wander aimlessly deep down in her self and then she had discovered on the boy's planet. It seemed as though, in that remote place, she had touched her dreams, which she was recognizing and making her own again on her own planet.

She was looking at the same sun and the same land through different eyes now, discovering that this inner world of hers had always been and continued to live inside her, no matter whether she had realized it before or not. Wherever she had been, whatever questions she had asked herself, this inner universe of hers had always existed, though imperceptible and misunderstood in the time of her trials and tribulations. She felt happy and clapped her hands.

As incredible as it might sound, she realized that this foreign land was an unknown planet, which was located deep inside her soul.

She didn't know which road led to travelling through time, far in the Universe to the unknown planet, but she knew it was also the road that led to the inner self of man. How was it possible to travel that far away and simultaneously to cover a reciprocal distance from the road to your inner self? How is it possible for the whole Universe to be printed inside us and whenever we discover a new planet, we carry inside us, discover yet another tiny part of who we really are. She was engulfed in those complicated matters and pondered over this controversial and irreconcilable logic.

She came to a surprising conclusion that since the planet lay somewhere in her soul, then the boy himself lived somewhere deep inside her. Perhaps it was like a stretch from an infinite line.

She wanted to summarize her thoughts and dreams scientifically and to try to define them. She assumed that she was the zero in a straight number line that is endless in length. Travelling to her dreams in space was like moving right from the zero towards the positive numbers and travelling to herself was like moving left from the zero towards the negative numbers. Irrespective of the direction she moved in, the reciprocal value of the numbers increased and only its sign would be different.

Depending on whether the numbers are positive or negative, they would be endlessly big or small. The same way as when, if hurled 500 000 km into outer space, equals diving deep into yourself to—500 000 km, which is the equivalent distance but it is covered in different ways and using different means for traveling through space and in your own body.

She already knew what it meant to reach a foreign planet, but she could also find this planet in herself now, where her dreams with the boy were lying. This new feeling of obtained knowledge gave her the happiness that she possessed everything she had ever needed, while striding content and smiling in her homeland. For her travelling didn't matter anymore, because it happened in two directions, or rather in two dimensions which collided inside of her and were part of the existence of her being.

She knew already what it took to reach the alien planet. This new sense of knowledge gave her the happiness she really needed to remain in her homeland.

She was convinced that the Earth, like the boy had rightly said, had separated into two halves. And believed that this created precisely those impulses in people to seek a home elsewhere, in a new or unknown place far away from where they were born.

She remembered how, while she had been dreaming of being strong, she would sometimes throw accusations at the others in an act of sheer helplessness. In her desire to be perfect she would often fail and that would give rise to her irritation—again directed at the others. She wanted to think with hope in her heart about the victory, without complaining or giving up, but her failures upset and discouraged her. That's why a feeling suddenly engulfed her and she wanted just to sit for a while and someone to wrap his arms around her, seeing in her the little beauty that she had even when she was weak. She needed the warmth of that hug, springing from a noble heart, which would pump new strength into her veins.

She tried hard to be strong, but she also needed someone who would give her that strength. She remembered the creator, who the people on the boy's planet worshipped and who they would always turn to with joyful awe and the strongest conviction that he was the primal source of their strength and abilities. They had that primeval source that would give them everything they needed so that their hearts could be full of joy, of which they would have enough for themselves and they would often give others.

Now she was just happy to be home where her soul belonged. She was in a world full of so many wonderful things that she felt secure, loved and free from anguish.

Sitting on her old shaggy couch was more or less like sitting on such thousands of spacious green lawns. When she sipped water from a cup, it was like sipping a clear spring from the high mountains. All her friends suddenly appeared to be extraordinary people who looked at her with special attention. Nothing seemed easy or simple but everything was unusual and miraculously worthy of her admiration. This made her enjoy things that previously went unnoticed.

As she sat down on a bench, she felt the urge to sit for hours to make up for lost time.

The couple in love that she often met taking a stroll down her street and who she used to secretly envy in the past, now seemed falsely in love, like a shiny wrapping but without any contents that would try to make up for that emptiness with glamour and panache. She had never seen them arguing and making up after that and his to her was only an illusion which they used in a futile attempt to conceal the gaping abyss between them, which was only growing larger and larger as the phoniness increased and through showing off with their possessions with which they were trying to fill in the lack of genuine sincerity between them. They also lacked the strength of dignity to confess to each other their weaknesses and despite these weaknesses to continue to love each other more and more with every passing day—over and over again. There was another couple of her relatives who she was disgusted with because of their daily rows that would constantly find their way into their relationship.

Couples strolled along the street, appearing lovelier than ever.

She wanted to swim, remembering that she could enjoy the water, which did not exist freely in its liquid form in the other land. Because of this, humidity now appeared delightful. This made her feel somehow closer to her goals, because they seemed to have been born somewhere here, on her planet. It seemed only natural to her that her dreams had found her and had managed to give her the gift of what made her truly happy without her chasing fake cravings that resembled her happiness. She felt that she could have everything because it started happening to her. The peace and calmness that reigned inside her gave her the wings to fly higher than all her dreams could take her, unsuspecting that it was possible for them to be more beautiful than her dreams themselves.

This peace inside her, she had brought from the other land together with the tiny seeds of which she has already sowed her own in a flowerpot on the terrace and the rest she had given away. She gave one to the couple in love, whose now looked unhappy, with the hope that the seed would bring them real happiness, the happiness she had always thought they had in the first place. Another seed she gave to the constantly arguing couple whose devotion to each other she had recently discovered. What was going to be born out of their seed? She didn't know for sure, but she was certain it would bring them different events and cravings that would make them happier and more loving towards each other.

She clearly remembered that when she had been given those seeds, she was told that they would grow and give different fruits, depending on the needs of those that sowed them and the fruits would be as delicious and ripe, as tender and loving as the care they had been grown with. She tried hard to be consistent and responsible in her daily care for the seed in her flower pot.

This peace she has brought from other land, along with those wonderful seeds already planted on the balcony, impatiently waiting for its fruits. She was eager to see the little seed protruding into a plant from a foreign planet, but now growing on her own land and on her balcony.

Otherland

Chapter 27

The Time Lost

After returning back to his planet, he started having mixed feelings. Accidentally his gloves fell on the ground and he bent to pick them up. Though he initially hated to wear gloves, he loved them because they were a gift from her and she urged him to warm his hands at least by putting them on. The weather started to change, but he continued wearing the gloves.

In the past he would carefully wipe out every single spot on his fancy ball-shaped car. Now even the enormous ice-cream smudge on top of it was left there after his cousin had accidentally dropped it, though seemed too small to notice. He didn't even notice the car itself. He walked these days, the longer the better, haunted by his memories of his strolls with the girl.

In the past he would insist on her loving him, understanding his world, loving his world and becoming a part of it, like everyone else here. And now he didn't like anyone on his planet because he constantly sought her eyes and was sad to find out that no one resembled her in the least.

In her world, everything was moving more slowly. People there loved differently and often hid from one other. For him she was different. He wanted her, not the world where she lived, because she was his world.

His friend approached and passed through their garden, hoping for another trip down to the river with his boat. This would only highlight more of the sadness about their separation, since they had spent the last moments together on the same boat. Then he remembered the bewilderment they had always had due to their differences. And he never complained about this, but now tears were in his eyes, and he rushed quickly to leave his friend who has failed to notice his sadness.

It was as if he was looking at the weeping eyes of the girl before him and she was looking at him with helpless sorrow because of all the pain of all the misunderstood and unspoken words, of the misplaced gestures or of the missed actions and moments which he had failed to give her the way she wanted him to. And all this arose from the differences, which stood in his way, to completely understand her.

This even prevented him from thanking her for the love she had given him because he had blurry vision and he couldn't see clearly, nor could he truly understand her. Filled with the habits of his land he lacked the conscience back then to protect and preserve close to him everything dear that she was giving him as her gift. Now he would remember her dreams and would weep, forgetting he was a man who should never whine and now it seemed that those were not his, but her tears, rolling down his cheeks.

He longed for turning back time. He wished that he could have been able to understand her better back then, before she had shed a single tear. He was not sure whether he was blaming himself or her sensitivity that allowed her to be so easily hurt by every mistake and misunderstanding. That made him feel as if he was putting the blame on her again, trying to exonerate himself. And that didn't make him feeling good, now hating the fear he had used so far to make excuses. He was ready to take the blame and he didn't want to make her cry again. He never wanted to make anyone cry.

How he wished to turn back time! He so much wished to have understood her better, to stop her from shedding all her own tears. For a moment this made him feel like blaming her, while at the same time trying to justify himself. This argument was a transparent attempt to evade taking the guilt. He now realised it was his obligation to protect her; until now he had longed for the power which could bring him admiration and obedience from others. But now the admiration or praises from others couldn't make him feel happy. Now he could only measure his powerfulness by how happy he could make her, or how much he could replace her tears with smiles.

His hands were strong. His muscles twitched in readiness to move, only to be paralyzed by his soul. He cried and fought with himself to admit his mistakes and remember her words.

He knew that so many tears could drown his conscience, since they were pouring not only over his face, but over his hands as well. The more his palms would get wet, the more he wanted to cry, filled with hope that he could dry his tears once and for all, but they kept streaming from his eyes. He was fighting his inner self, but he knew he missed her dearly and he had to confess it. Her words made him numb. The words his mind reminded him of and he understood that they were very right and he was the one who had misinterpreted them before. Guilt—that was all he would admit to himself. It hurt to see himself so guilty.

Everything was just about her. And losing her meant losing his world and its tangible assets. He looked around and noticed that nothing he had left behind would bring any delight or satisfaction to him.

Even his plane was not as dear to him now as it had been before. He didn't want to make excuses for himself anymore because he felt like the biggest coward alive and unworthy of embracing what he was dreaming of and it was not only her. He was ready to take the blame and admit he was guilty. He would admit it to his soul, to his heart, to his land because he wanted her to smile again. He had lost everything he once thought he possessed, because he had lost her and she meant more to him than anything else. He was a burden to himself and nothing of what he had turned into would bring him admiration or content. He wanted to be everything she had longed for.

Previous wishes were no longer important. His breath and every other thing appeared very old, unlike before, making him feel like a foreigner in his own land, without any desire to belong to his world again. He had seen another world which brought about the abrupt U-turn. The fact remained clear. The truth kept burning and his bones were unable to escape from it. Though the blaze was invisible, the burn could be easily seen in his eyes. He regretted ever allowing her departure. He acknowledged also, that living away from her had disrupted his days.

His entire planet ground to a halt. Clocks stopped ticking and the only thing that kept him alive was memories of those moments they had shared. He was pushed to stop loving everything he had ever loved before. His eyes were hungry to see her, his hands were useless.

More than anything he wanted to love her in the earthly manner she had dreamed of, so that she could understand and believe him. He wanted to give her everything she had wanted in order to prove to her that his love is endless and his greatest happiness was the one she could make come true if she wished to come back into his life and kiss him with her love.

He started crying again, but not because he felt pity for himself or because of the burning craving for her tenderness, but because of the desire and hope that in that way, though it was rather foggy how, he would wipe away all her tears shed in the past. He found the lies he had used to excuse himself and to deceive her. He knew that he had hurt her with those lies and now he had to pay the high price of this madness which hurt him innumerable times as much as he had hurt her.

The universe was no longer so beautifully desirable, without her beauty. He became thoughtful for a moment, remembering their first meeting. They met, introduced themselves and later travelled together, spending such wonderful moments together as well as stepping up their love's meteoric rise. In spite of all this, he still felt resentful and depressed for her tears and the time lost, time he could have spent making her happy. Although she was not there, all his heart belonged to her.

She was his happiness which he was longing to find again. That seemed impossible, but even more impossible was the sorrow to breathe without her. Although she was gone, his whole heart belonged to her forever. He was achingly in love and had madly separated with that love. He wanted to fight, but he didn't know how. He was searching those different and new things on his planet which existed on the girl's Earth, but they remained only there because they were related to her.

He knew he had to return back to the Earth at any cost.

He began with his preparation for a journey back to Earth.

He took some special nuts which he hoped to plant on Earth, where he would build his castle, because her heart is the only place in the world where he can feel at home, and a king.

Chapter 28

A Journey Together

The trip back to earth was chaotic, as he was so eager to arrive there, this makes him failed to notice when he finally got down to her beloved planet. He began to look for her.

The city, streets and houses were similar to those in his homeland and this had contributed to facilitating navigation in finding her home. Even though both homes had much in common, he was able to notice some elements of difference in the houses.

Both lands were parallel worlds with similar structures. This perhaps made their souls closer irrespective of the distance between the two planets, which had been one planet many years back.

After a long period of frustration and anticipation, he finally arrived at her home only to meet her absence. Her neighbour told him she had left some hours ago for an unknown place. He thought perhaps she had gone to the river for a walk, knowing very well how much she loved such places while she was in his planet. He set out for her river.

On the unfamiliar way he realised that he felt lost in both universes, unsure where he belonged. Fears and anxiety encompassed his whole being and he couldn't figure out how to confront the huge challenges ahead.

The same changes happened to the girl herself. She didn't perceive her homeland the same way, nor did she like the same things she had liked before. When she returned from the planet of the boy, she was looking to recognize many things on her planet that would resemble the things she had found in the foreign land. But she couldn't find the same things, that's why she was carrying some kind of sadness in her and mostly she would feel sad because she missed the boy, trying to recognize him in the faces she met. However, she couldn't find anyone that looked like him.

So when she saw him coming, she was excited but confused at the same time by his unexpected appearance, and by not knowing whether he would stay. This confusion made her quickly dive into the water in order to hide herself there.

For him, his heart was filled with excitement after seeing her swimming. Nevertheless he was still at a crossroad, struggling within his soul. And she looked so different too, compared with the last time he kissed her on his planet.

In fact, both seemed appeared unlike the way they had previously known themselves; again it appeared they were meeting for the first time. But this time they were not sure if they could still acknowledge the love which both had earlier embraced.

Thus they remained tight-lipped, staring at each other with such different eyes. He was startled by fear, which later shifted into sadness, repressed weaknesses and other shortcomings. But he had been dreaming of this moment since he left her. Now that she was there in the water before him, he desired not to miss this opportunity to tell her how he felt.

Before he could stop himself, he dove into the water and began to swim. She stared at him. He wasted no time in embracing her and seeking her forgiveness. He kept pressing her firmly until both got obsessed by their body language and started talking between the lines. After kissing him, she told him how much she had missed him.

Their kiss was a miracle. Both were extremely generous. They stared at each other and from that point rediscovered their togetherness. They travelled together to both lands and realized that they shared a common planet, divided by distance. Their common home was their hearts that had merged.

Wherever they travelled, they felt home, hugging with the love and the tender care they felt for each other. Sinking in his eyes, the girl found for the first time the secret that unraveled before her very eyes. The boy was getting dearer and dearer to her, bringing the memories of her childhood dreams that had been forgotten long ago, hidden somewhere deep down in her and hopelessly rejected.

In her dream, was a little boy who had always smiled at her while she wondered about what love was. She was certain now he was the same boy that had appeared in her dream. She had loved this unknown boy even when she was little, even in her dreams.

Surprised and happy, almost unable to believe her eyes, which also embraced his smile, she knew already that dreams once dreamed could be found and could stay in one's life forever. Thus they could make you happier than when you had been dreaming those dreams.

Epilogue

Your home is where your choice is!
The land kisses the sea with a clash.
The clash shatters planets and civilizations.
It meets and separates people, changing their dreams.
The clash begets the fear of the unknown, hidden in the changes, but the clash also changes you and recreates you, reaching out a helping hand to all your fears.
The clash meets one with love, but also faces them with Death.
The clash creates with its destruction and for this reason takes you back to where you had been trying to escape from.
After the clash you may find yourself loving what you had thought you had hated before, to hear the truth where there had always been silence and to hug the person whom you had never noticed passing by.
But mostly your personal happiness awakes to life when you clash with your own dreams.

Dide

Otherland

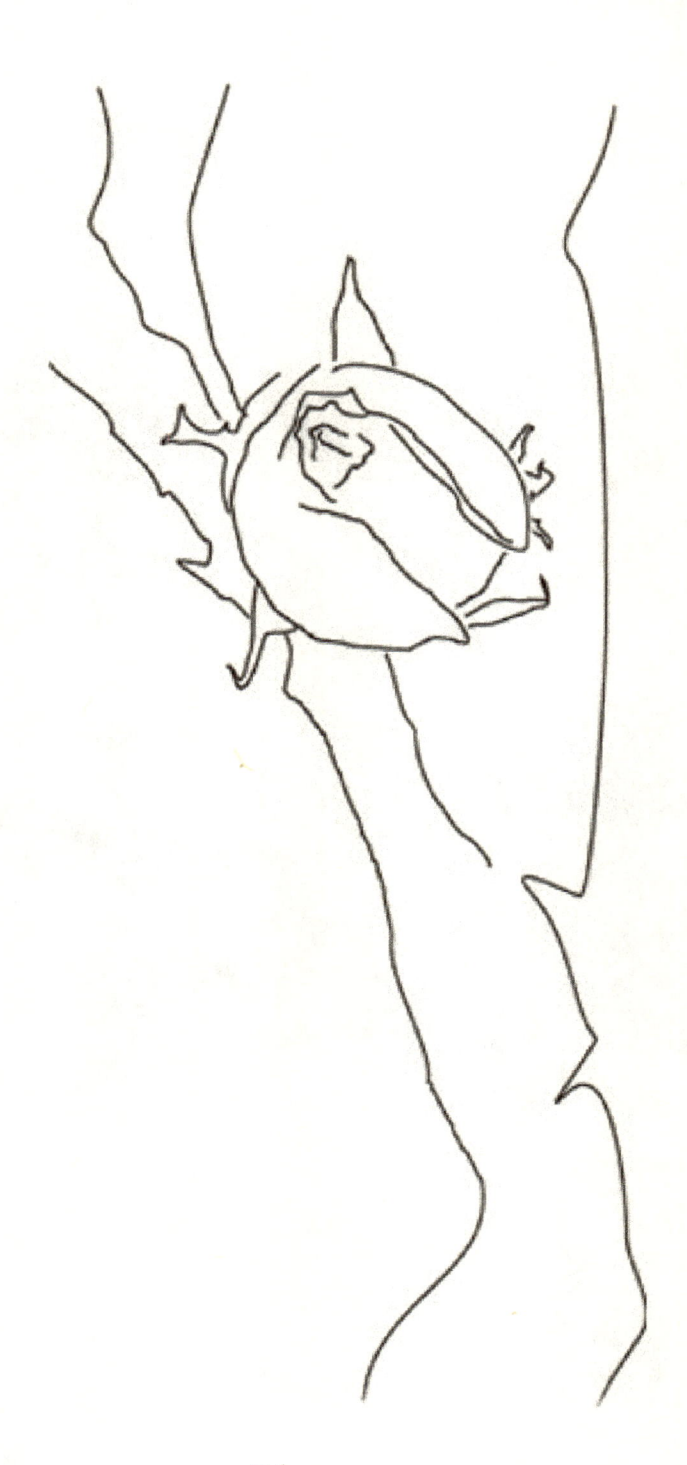

Dide

Printed in the USA
CPSIA information can be obtained
at www.ICGtesting.com
LVHW090838041224
798224LV00018BA/142/J